Art of the Genre represents a huge shared world called *The Nameless Realms*, a place that spans thirteen extraordinary Ages of Man. Each category of fiction in this fantastic world has its own specialized medallion that is 'active' in the upper right corner of each book, thus allowing you to easily tell what specific genre you're purchasing. In the case of **The Mid-Winter Fall**, you're about to enter the 5th age of Man, in a setting of Adventure Fantasy, so the medallion you see above is the symbol for all books in that field.

THE
MID-WINTER FALL

THE FIVE YEAR WAR: VOLUME TWO

SCOTT TAYLOR

Illustrated by
JEFF EASLEY
KEITH PARKINSON
TIMOTHY TRUMAN
JIM HOLLOWAY
LARRY ELMORE

The Mid-Winter Fall
Copyright © 2013 Art of the Genre

Printed and bound in the United States of America 9 8 7 6 5 4 3 2 1

First edition: March 2013

ISBN: 978-0-9857674-9-5

This is a work of fiction. All characters, places and events portrayed in this publication are either fictitious or used fictitiously.

Cover: Jeff Easley
Interior Illustrations: Jeff Easley, Keith Parkinson, Timothy Truman, Jim Holloway, and Larry Elmore
Copy Editor Extreme: Joshua Villines
Graphic Design: Jeff Laubenstein
Cartography: Alyssa Faden
Book Design: John Woolley
My Writing Instructor: Terri-Lynne DeFino
Sounding Board: John O'Neill

Art of the Genre
217 Palos Verdes Blvd,
Redondo Beach, CA 90277

artofthegenre.myshopify.com

Ordering Information:
For details, contact the publisher at the address above.

I'm going to dedicate this book to two people.

First, to a middle-school teacher who tried to make a club for Dungeons & Dragons in the mid-80s but was thoroughly defeated by the parents of the school. To Mr. Keiser, even though your club only lasted two months, it has given me nearly 30 years of joy, friendships, and profitable and fulfilling work that I could never have imagined without your help in getting me started.

And to my oldest role-playing friend, and DM to end all DMs, Mark Timm. Words can never describe what your friendship and imagination has meant to me. Without you none of this would have been possible, and I thank you from the bottom of my heart for always being there, no matter what adventure my sometimes scattered brain decided I needed to undertake.

I also have to once again thank all the fans on Kickstarter who made this dream a reality with their generous donations. Because of fans like you, Art of the Genre managed to produce five novels with fantastic old school artists in 2012, and that is a feat you should all be proud of.

CONTENTS

FOREWORD

The Mid-Winter Fall is the culmination of a gaming campaign that ended just before the turn of the millennia. It was an experience I'll never forget, and having the chance to bring fans of old school RPG novels and art along in the process was as rewarding as any I've ever had.

This book takes place directly after the events in *The Cursed Legion*, and I guess it could be called the second half of a duology, a term coined by Dennis L. McKiernan when he wrote *Trek to Kraggen-Cor* and *The Brega Path*.

I know I can never rise to the level of those masterful books, but I hope that those of you who have invested in this book enjoy what I've written. Make no mistake, an incredible amount of care went into this creation, and I can't tell you how thrilled I am to bring you original artwork by legendary TSR artists Jeff Easley, Keith Parkinson, Timothy Truman, Jim Holloway, and Larry Elmore. I'd also like to thank Nick Parkinson and Donna Parkinson for providing unpublished sketches of Keith's work that Timothy Truman could finish for this project.

I know for a fact, this is the only time in history that original work from all of these artists has appeared in a single volume, be it literature or gaming supplement.

So take heed, and get ready to set forth on adventure like you were at the gaming table. The Mid-Winter War is in full swing, and the exploits of Erik, Saffron, Relan, and even Igrayn awaits!

Scott Taylor
January 2013

ACKNOWLEDGEMENTS

Andy Molloy, Chris Baker, pratchettfan, Brandon Haase,
Justin Larsen, Joseph Hoopman, Chiara Pasquini, Jason Stockmann

Katherine 'KatKat' Schramm, V. 'Trit' Reid, Dani Akiyama,
Graham Harper, Renzo Crispieri, Gwendolyn McIntyre,
Michael Mock, Luke Gygax, Matthew Wood

Matthew Gushta, Thom Walls

Steven J. Landseadel, James Lewis, Magentawolf, Garry Jenkins,
Martyn Warren, Kent Rice, Michael 'NightWind' Mair, Aaron W,
Jason Azze

Mikael Olofsson, Chris Thompson, Kyle Pinches

Eric Shofe, Paul Jarman, Grubnash, Michael Hurwood,
Andrew Findlay, Michael 'Rhel' Green, David Chamberlain,
Sarah Gruetze, Paul Arneil, Karl 'the Good' Thiebolt,
Francis Morehouse, Tim Cahoon, Ingrid Emilsson

Peter M. Poulsen

Brett 1324, Benny Hsieh, Michael Lewis

The Nameless Realms: The Country of Aflyr

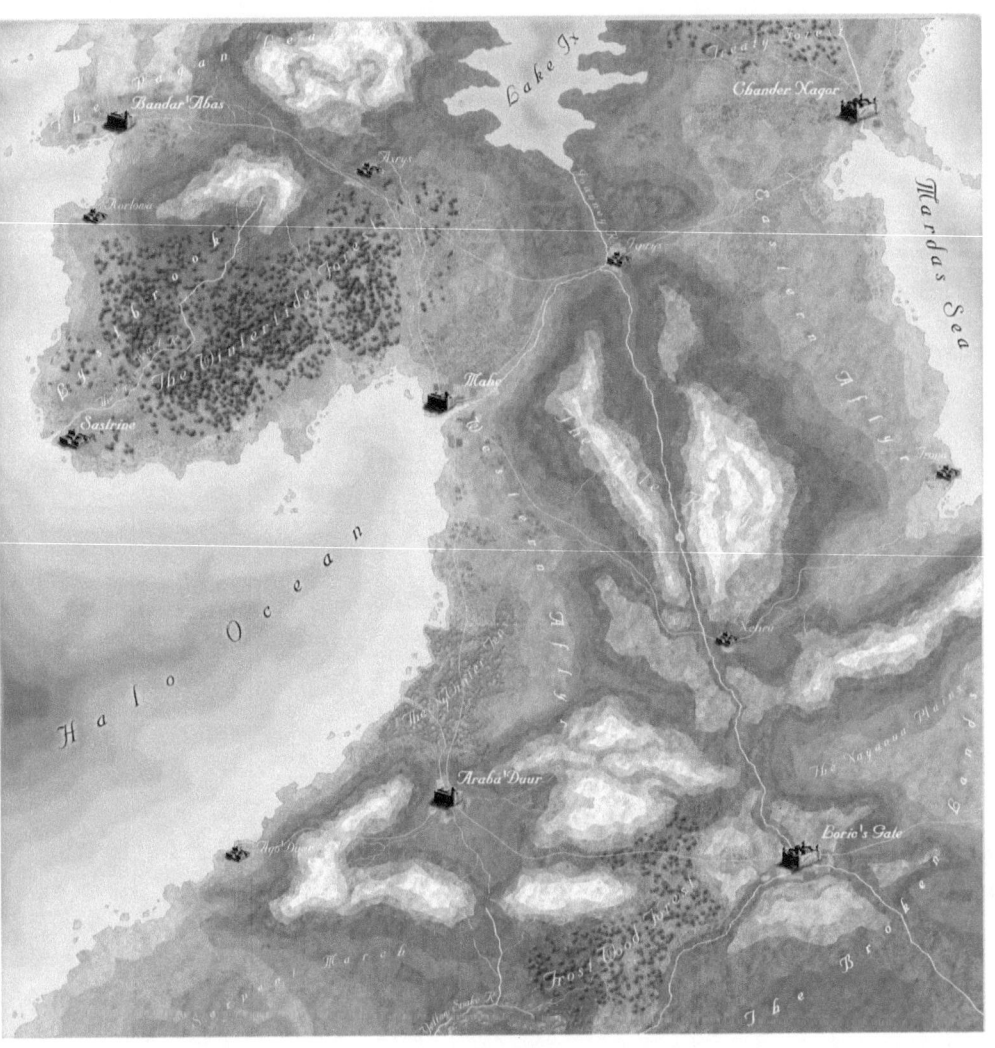

THE
MID-WINTER FALL

BOOK I

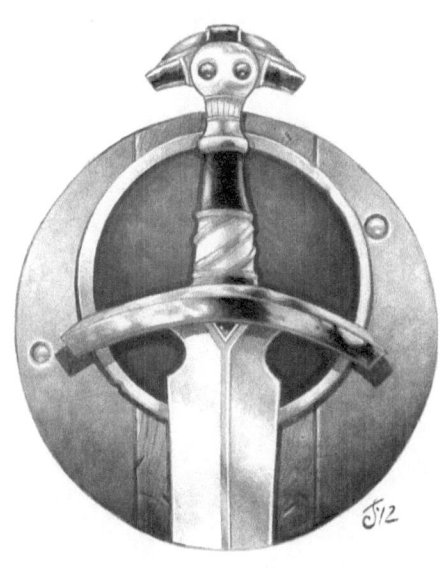

CHAPTER ONE

RELAN AND SAFFRON

*D*o *you believe I'm outside the bounds of my responsibility? I know it's a question that lurks within your mind, the tendrils of it washing against my thoughts like waves against the shore.*

Perhaps you're right, but I will make this journey nonetheless, and when it is done you can set your final judgment upon me and I will accept the verdict without plea or retort.

The shadow of death now resides on my hands, the stain untenable unless I find a purpose to it greater than the loss of half a hundred trees. That is my way, and I must keep to my convictions or be lost inside the maelstrom of guilt for the remainder of my days...

Saffron groaned, a subtle warmth trickling over her cheeks. She drew a blanket deep beneath her chin and turned slightly, chainmail biting her in the shoulder.

"Gods!" she cried.

Sitting up, she reached for her blade but grabbed only air. Around her, pale sunlight slipped in misty columns from a crumbled ceiling and a golden glow burned near her from the end of a staff.

"Be at peace, Corsair, there is no threat to you here," a voice said.

She turned, the figure of a man taking shape as her eyes adjusted to the brightness of the staff and the shadows beyond it.

"Where am I?" she asked.

"The Wintertide," he replied.

"Where's my sword?"

"A dangerous weapon, that. Why do you carry it?"

She tried to rise but the earthen, leaf-covered floor held her, roots having grown around her legs and torso.

Druid!

"I have no reason to confide in you, forest warden," she answered.

"That may be true in your home, but in the Wintertide you are under the laws of the Druid's Council, and therefore have no rights at all."

She pulled once, fiercely, at her bonds. They held tight. She let out a long breath, asking, "To what purpose do you hold me?"

"I hold you because there is a foul threat about these lands, something that has bled its way from Lystbrook into this forest, and you would seem to be a part of it."

She stared at him. He was tan-skinned, a tangle of unkempt brown hair hanging about his lean face and several ivory-decorated braids fell past his leather-clad shoulders. The room smelled of fire, and wind moved about in odd bursts. She could feel the Druid's mixed nature washing over her water spark.

"I've recently come from Lystbrook, and I would agree there is a darkness there I've not seen in the past," she said.

He nodded, pointing to her left, and she followed his direction. Beside her, a cup made of pasted leaves sat amid a collection of onions, strips of dark dried meat, and cracked walnuts.

Her stomach grumbled, and she reached out to take a piece of meat. It held little taste, but she swallowed it down with water and then started on an onion.

"You speak of darkness," he began, "but can you tell me what that really means?"

"There is a problem with the nobility," she answered.

"What kind of problem?"

She turned to look at him more closely. One of his eyes was cobalt blue, the other amber.

What have you seen, Druid, that has brought you so close to the lands of humanity?

"I thought Druids didn't get involved in the affairs of human kingdoms?" she asked.

"When humanity invades the Wintertide, involvement by my order is unavoidable."

"Invasion?" she asked.

"Two days ago I destroyed an army from Lystbrook that were setting siege to a forest keep deep within the wood," he answered.

She tried to rise again, but the roots held her.

Damn the gods, what game is this?

"What army?" she demanded.

"One carrying the Kingfisher of Lystbrook at its head and championed by the crown prince."

Wilam.

"What do you mean you 'destroyed' it?" she asked.

"As I said, the army is no more."

She shook her head, "And the prince?"

"To me there are only men. Rank means nothing, and so he suffered the same fate as the rest."

There was a long silence, the pulsing of the three firebirds on the Druid's staff the only motion, until she spoke again.

"What will you do now?" she asked.

"I will journey to Sastrine and I will discern the cause of this invasion."

"And I will go with you," she added.

He tilted his head, "Why would you do that?"

"I am Saffron of Grey Banks, Shield Maiden to Princess Ergoroth, and I believe that the royal family has been corrupted."

"Including your princess?" he asked.

She shook her head, "No, Igrayn was sent away months ago. I couldn't figure out why until now. I believe something has happened, and that the family is under attack."

"By whom?"

"I don't know, but if it is in my power, I'm going to find out."

The Druid nodded and sat back, his voice even, "Then you should eat. It will be a long walk tomorrow, and the winter is coming quickly."

CHAPTER TWO

ERIK

One moment you're a court dandy, the next a planar rogue, then a bodyguard, a mercenary, and finally a knight.

I guess in all this, that might be the reason you watch over me, at least because my life seems to be anything but boring.

So now I lead men, cavalrymen to be precise, down into the southlands and the hill country toward Nehru Fortress. Old Nehru, a bastion as cold as an old woman's...well, you get the idea. I thought I'd gotten rid of the place months ago when I picked up Braxus and Malcolm, but now I return.

At least this time I have company, and I'm on a purpose greater than fleeing the bounty hunters and rogues who seek to make a gold coin off passing on my whereabouts. Still, if I wanted to stay hidden – and surely I do – I shouldn't be riding a steed and sporting a shining helm and steel-tipped lance.

If only I could control that part of me that wants what it wants and is willing to send the rest of creation to the Nine Hells to get it. As Shera would say, 'you are what you are, and the sooner you accept that, the easier life will be.' Perhaps she's right, but nothing about what I'm currently doing seems remotely easy...

Erik wheeled his steed around and took the head off a fleeing Delver, *Fury* flashing in the morning sun. Around him more men on horseback lanced and cut the Delver raiding party to ribbons, while a collection of sallow-faced villagers cheered them on from behind their makeshift barricades.

Erik spurred his stallion on, a Jai-Ruk commander bracing to take his charge. The massive creature raised his scimitar, his raw element filling the battlefield with the stink of the deep earth. Their weapons clashed, and Erik pulled hard on the reins. His warhorse reared and planted a hoof against the helm of the Jai-Ruk, sending him staggering back with his helm bent over his nose. Erik turned his mount, and ran his blade across the Jai-Ruk's armored shoulders until it caught under a plate and cut deeply into flesh.

The Ruk tumbled forward, and Erik's mount leapt onto him, crushing his bones into the half-frozen field with a clatter of metal on metal.

"Erik!" Braxus called, his light brown warhorse fighting against its reins amid the melee.

"What?" Erik shouted back as he left the Ruk corpse behind and galloped to his lieutenant.

"A half dozen have gotten into the southern buildings of the village, and smoke's beginning to rise over there.

Braxus pointed with his sword toward the black smoke pluming up in the far side of the village.

Thunder boomed and blue lightning shattered the battlefield as Telluria unleashed unchained *Afterglow* from her newly acquired staff. Where the bolt struck, a dozen Delvers were cast asunder like children's dolls, their smoking remains dropping into a tight knot of Jai-Ruk defense.

Somewhere to the south a Delver war horn blew and Erik saw a line of lancers turning in that direction with Malcolm at their head. The mercenary had donned a suit of half-plate taken from the palace armory, and he wielded a long-bladed lance that rose above those of his fellow cavaliers.

"Malcolm has them. Where's Igrayn?" Erik asked.

"Here!" Igrayn called from behind him.

Her riding mare had been replaced with a stout, black and white warhorse, and she wore a bright chain shirt and visored half-helm etched with eagle wings. Sabre in hand, she gave Tavalori a nod as he rode up next to her, only one of his three quivers of red-fletched arrows still full.

A grin slid across Erik's lips before he asked, "You're starting to enjoy this aren't you?"

Her bright green eyes held his a moment, the smell of the ocean mixing with the tang of blood, before she looked away, saying, "Don't get too carried away and think you can speak to me thus, 'Sir' Tall Hills."

Tavalori frowned and Ash leaned around him to provide a smile. "They seem to be getting along rather well, wouldn't you say, Tavalori?" the Eldaryn asked.

Heat bloomed about the two, Tavalori's horse throwing its head back and forth before more horns sounded from his lancer vanguard. A collection of bronze-plated cavalry was pursuing a routed group of Delvers from the west village, and Erik sat back in his saddle.

"Another village saved," he sighed, more than a hint of pride in his voice.

Igrayn pulled her horse closer and leaned toward him.

"You really do care about these people, don't you?" she whispered. He was about to reply when Braxus' wild horse got between Tavalori and the princess, making the young woodsman curse as he pulled his steed back away from the group.

Erik turned to her, his spark alight in his chest, "I actually do..."

"Then I believe the knighthood suits you," she said before her eyes went back to the barricades where people were already coming out cheering the riders on.

Erik laughed, "And I bet there will be some very grateful young women in this village!"

He spurred his horse forward, and after a moment's pause Igrayn did the same, the two of them racing toward the town as Tavalori called for them to wait. They were in full flight, and the chaotic litter of corpses, armor, and weapons put the horsemanship of both riders to the test.

When the two frothing horses finally pulled up before a group of wide-eyed villagers, Erik was laughing, his spark in full bloom.

"Milord, Milady," called one of the men, his bulk as heavy as the sledgehammer he carried over his shoulder.

Erik concealed his smile and bound his laughter, but the villagers were nonetheless dark in their expressions as he slid off the saddle.

He gave a slight whistle as he was looked up a full six inches to the man's bearded chin. The huge warrior was at least seven feet, bald-pated and grim in his leathers and furs.

"I'm Sir Erik Tall Hills, and you are?" Erik asked.

"The name is Cronin of Calpcon and these are my men," the giant answered.

Erik looked around the man's shoulder at a collection of a dozen rough looking men who were armed with all manner of weapons.

"Cronin? And you're from this village?" Erik asked.

Cronin shook his great head, his beard wagging as he did so. His coat of heavy, boiled leather and his animal skin cloak made him look near as wide as he was tall.

"No, my village was in the highlands, but it was put to the torch three weeks past. I, and some survivors, have been hunting this band of Delvers while trying to help where we could," Cronin answered.

Erik raised an eyebrow, "That's noble of you."

"Nothing noble about it, Milord. We have a debt to pay to those that took our families, and we mean to see it done," Cronin said.

Erik gave a nod, saying, "As these Delvers have been destroyed, I would offer you a further chance to find some revenge elsewhere. My lancers and I travel south by the old sea road to the coastal towns and then on to the Yule Ranges making our way to the Fortress at Nehru. I've heard tell the fortress is besieged, and I'm looking for strong men to help me free the place when I arrive."

Cronin shook his head, "My men will never match the speed you will make on those mounts, Milord."

"Indeed, that's why I would ask you to take your men across the foothills from here and meet me just west of the Tall Hills pass. If we're lucky, we should make it to those white tops around the same time," Erik said.

"There would be a great deal of luck in either of us getting to Tall Hills, what with winter nearly on and so many Delvers in the land, but I've no place else to go, nor do my men." Cronin answered.

Malcolm's cavalry unit appeared from the west, Delver heads placed on their lances and grim smiles showing beneath helms.

Tavalori, Braxus, and Ash came up then as well, Ash lamenting the difficulty of firing from horseback.

Erik offered Cronin his hand, "Very well, Cronin, I will see you in Tall Hills, and together we'll find the cause of this invasion and continue our purpose to do right by the people."

Cronin nodded, shook Erik's hand, and then turned back to talk with his men. Other folk from the town came forward, mostly older men, and shook Erik's hand or patted him on the shoulder. He smiled, provided answers to questions, and looked behind the vanguard at the women who waited there.

Certainly there must be a warm bed within this town where I can rest for an evening...

"Sir Tall Hills?" Igrayn asked.

He turned back to her, "Yes?"

"I see no more Delvers from my vantage, so perhaps it's best we leave these people to right the wrongs done to their village," she said.

"The men have been hard afield. I think these people will provide warmth, food, and perhaps some hearth companionship this evening," he replied.

Igrayn's eyes grew narrow and she cast a look at Tavalori, saying, "If that is your wish, then perhaps fun and companionship might be had by all..."

You think to threaten me with Tavalori once more? If you want the young woodsman, have him, but you'll not trap me without proper bait, and that you haven't yet offered.

"As you will," he replied.

Turning, he took one of the town's elders by the shoulder and walked away, his course leading toward three young women watching the discussion from the front of a stable. Behind him, the smell of the ocean washed over his back and tickled his nose.

Two days had passed since the fight at Lowman's Stead and Igrayn hadn't spoken a word to him. Neither had Tavalori, who always had either Braxus or Ash close to by his side. The young woodsman carried a dark look, and his fire always burned with a hint of something strange in the essence.

Erik sat on a blanket, a fire burning at his feet and a single flap of canvas poled at his back to break the wind that trailed in off the marches. Beyond his fire, the similar open flames of his men burned as the company rested outside Kelp's Cross, scattered villagers still among them helping to tend to the evenings meal and give continued thanks for their assistance earlier in the day.

His horse, SmokeShadow, was tethered to a tree nearby, and it began to stamp the ground. Turning, he laid his hand on the hilt of *Fury* and got to his feet.

Where are Braxus and Malcolm when I need them?

"Who goes?" he called.

A tall shadow moved from the trees, his bulk unmistakable.

"Cronin?" Erik asked.

"It will be a long and cold night, Sir Tall Hills," Cronin answered.

Erik looked around, but no one else was near them, the closest canvas tent some thirty feet. The trees were dark and the Ghost Moon was obscured by a bank of passing clouds.

"Do you often lurk in the shadows when you should be miles into the eastern foothills?" Erik asked.

The giant man had his hammer resting on his shoulder, but he didn't threaten as he moved further into the evening shadow so that Erik could see him fully.

"No, but I do need to know what kind of man I would serve," he replied.

"And have you found that knowledge this evening?" Erik asked.

Cronin gave a grunt, "I heard that you accepted only minimal replenishment supplies from the villages you've saved, and tonight I saw you walk among your men bolstering their spirits. This is not something readily done by the nobility I've ever known in the lowlands," Cronin replied.

Erik scratched his chin, the growth there becoming sufficiently long after a week and a half on campaign outside Mahe.

"I find that my place is always better served in the company of my men than in a planner's tent, and a hungry army is a more dangerous one," Erik replied.

Cronin laughed at the last, "Tall Hills must be a land of fine nobility, although I know that your claim to hail from there has to be a lie."

You've been following me, but where are your men? I pray you've sent them on to Tall Hills because I'll need there number after losing twenty-two of my lancers since the city.

"Should I take offense at that?" Erik asked.

Cronin shook his head, "Not at all, Sir knight. I'm simply saying that you are a good leader, and if someone were to ask me about Tall Hills, I'd tell them that an ancient and just family is known to rule over it."

These people are desperate for leadership, first the Legion and now these hillmen. I have to wonder what kind of fool rules in ChanderNagor.

"If that's so, then we are in agreement that the people are in need of protection and that we are the ones to do it?" Erik asked.

Cronin nodded his thick head, "Yes, and I'll find more blades for you, as will my men before we get to Tall Hills."

"Well, for what it's worth, I have a feeling we'll need every one of those blades before this is done."

Cronin nodded and then walked away, his boots crunching the frosted earth. Erik sighed, his heat seeping from his shoulders as he moved back to his tent. The fire was now embers, and he threw two more pieces of wood on it, the tents of Braxus and Malcolm still empty and the other members of the company having taken refuge in the town's single inn.

I always tried to avoid my tactical studies because I was sure I'd never need them. I'm sure my old instructors would be having a good laugh right now if they could see me...

"Is this how knights spend their evenings?"

He turned. Igrayn was standing between Braxus and Malcolm's tents. She wore a heavy fur-lined cloak, her riding boots disappearing in the long folds as she tucked her arms around her chest.

She looks like a winter queen from an ancient legend.

"If it is, I wasn't told about it when I signed up," he replied.

She walked forward, tendrils of mist rising from her mouth as she spoke, "Where does one sign up to be a knight exactly?" she asked.

"Well, in Mahe I guess," he answered.

Kneeling down, she slipped into the wind-break of his canvas and pulled her cloak tighter around her shoulders.

Gods, what is this? First not a word and now a private meeting under moonlight? Her games never seem to end.

"Where is Tavalori?" he asked.

"You'd have to ask Ash, since he won't seem to leave his side," she answered.

"I've noticed."

She sighed, "So has he, but if he loses Ash, Braxus is right there to replace him."

"I'm not sure what those two are up to," Erik said.

"If you ask me, you put them up to it since you knew I wanted him."

He looked at her, and she turned to stare at him, her green eyes shining in the firelight.

"What benefit would I gain from such a thing?" he asked.

"You tell me?"

They stared at each other a long moment, his spark jumping about in his chest and her water seeping into his nose. He started to lean in, her breath so close he could taste its warmth, but Braxus appeared with a jingle of chainmail and they broke apart.

Breathless, the mercenary spoke, "Looks like all the lines are secure, the pickets are set, and the town has placed lookouts on the two grain towers."

Erik pulled away and nodded, "Very good."

Igrayn got to her feet and Braxus straightened up.

"Braxus, you've got a knack for appearing when you are least wanted," she said.

He smiled a gap-toothed grin.

"But, at least you've solved a bit of a mystery tonight," she continued.

"Miss?" Braxus asked.

She looked back at Erik, "You seem to be as determined at keeping me away from all men, not just Tavalori."

Braxus shook his head, "I don't know what you mean."

Moving around the mercenary, she exited the firelight, her voice drifting back to them, "Good night, Sir Tall Hills, and no matter what you might think, you're more noble than you give yourself credit."

Great, that makes twice tonight, another month of this play acting and I'll be raised to a kingship.

"What was that about?" Braxus asked.

Erik frowned, "You tell me?"

"What?"

"First you're ready to slip a dagger into Raziel because I've got an itch to scratch with Igrayn, and now you show up and stop something that I'm pretty sure was going to be the best thing to happen to me in months," Erik said.

"Now Erik, you know I wouldn't do that. I was just looking to get my report to you," Braxus replied, almost convincingly.

"Right, and I'm supposed to believe that? Do I look that gullible?"

Braxus sighed, looked left and then right, before he whispered, "It's not like that."

"Then what's it like?" Erik asked.

"I had a dream…"

"A dream?"

Braxus nodded, "Right, but not any dream, this one had Ash in it."

Erik waved his hands, "By the gods, I don't even want to know!"

"No, no, it wasn't like that!"

There was a long pause, Braxus staring at the fire before he continued, "Bandylegs was in it too."

"The god?"

"I swear its true, and he made both of us promise to see Igrayn…" he trailed off.

"Igrayn what?" Erik asked.

"Whole and virginal till her wedding day."

Erik spat, then said, "You think a god came to you in a dream and told you to keep a princess's maidenhead intact?"

Braxus was ashen, "I didn't at first, but then Ash started acting funny around her and when I mentioned my dream…"

"He'd had the same one?"

"Yeah!"

"You know he's a priest of Bandylegs and he's probably playing some huge joke on you, right?"

"It's real, I can almost feel Bandylegs watching me," Braxus said proclaimed indignantly

The mercenary looked around at the darkness as the wind picked up and both men burrowed deeper down inside their cloaks.

Yes, my friend, I know the feeling of being watched.

"So you're seriously going to protect her from herself?" Erik asked.

Braxus nodded, "What other choice do I have?"

I can think of several but I'll keep them to myself.

"Then good luck to you, I hope you and Ash are very happy together."

Braxus sighed, looked to say something else, bottled up, and then went beneath his tent as two sentries moved past, their spears catching the light of the fire.

This certainly adds a new fold, and it reaffirms my faith that gods should stay out of the lives of mortal men.

CHAPTER THREE

RELAN AND SAFFRON

As a shield maiden I have certain duties, the primary of them is to protect my princess. How I can do that while moving further away from her isn't fully known, and yet I march along with this Druid, both our destinies somehow linked with the insanity that has befallen the Lystbrook throne.

You are watching this, and yet you bring me no answer, frustrating me further. I crave something to fight, some enemy to vanquish, and yet I walk slowly west, the winter nipping at my heels.

Whatever comes, I will never forget my duty, or Igrayn. I will serve her till my last breath bleeds away, on that the gods can be certain.

"There should be people," Saffron said.

Relan didn't answer as he moved beside her, his staff aglow and the fields white with a fresh layer of frost.

"Do you hear me?" she asked.

"Yes, but it avails nothing to speak on a subject that is so abundantly clear," he replied.

Letting out a breath, she watched it rise as a white mist from her lips. Seven farmsteads lay behind them, all abandoned. Ahead, the scattered buildings of the city of Sastrine lay without a single wisp of chimney smoke disturbing the shining towers of morning light.

The Green Gift River flowed between the small city's northern and southern districts, three bridges spanned the flow, but not a single boat plied the water or raised white sail as it entered the bay.

I've been gone less than a week and the city is dead. What curse has come to my home while I was away?

Upon Noble Hill the Lystbrook Castle stood, its twin keeps spreading around the base of the rise, leading to a single tower that rose up above all else at the summit to overlook the waters of the western Halo Ocean.

"People were here as recently as two days past, but they've gone, most of them having travelled north," Relan said.

"How can you know that?" she asked.

"I can smell them on the wind, feel their elements drifting in the breeze. There is fear in it," he answered.

"Why? Why would they go?"

"Men come from across the water, their scent mixed with oil and steel," Relan answered.

"What?" she asked.

He didn't reply, just continued on his slow march. She drew close to him, her fingers flexing in her gloves and the smell of the sea drifting in the air.

"Are you saying there is an invasion coming? From where?" she demanded.

"I cannot say," he replied.

"Give me my sword!"

He stopped and she almost ran into him before she pulled back. He turned to her, his cloak and hair almost fully concealing his face.

"What use have you for a sword where an army is concerned?" he asked.

"I can fight!"

"I have no doubt, but against such a foe one blade, no matter how enchanted, cannot hope to stand," he replied.

The tang of salt hung in the air and she drew close, but he placed his staff between them. The three firebirds at the head flared until she covered her eyes.

"What purpose have you here, what goal do you truly seek?" he asked.

"I seek the truth!"

"And you think it takes a sword to find the truth?"

She took a step back, the heat from the staff drawing water from her hands and face.

Relan continued, "Will you fight a building? Will stone and mortar tell you a tale?"

"I've got to do something!" she shouted in response.

The light vanished, and she blinked, Relan staring at her as she caught her breath.

"The blade is dangerous, yet you would have it back?" he asked.

She nodded, "Yes."

He reached inside his cloak and withdrew her sabre, the edge catching the morning light.

"Not everyone has left the city, I sense that the tower is still occupied, perhaps your King awaits the arrival of his new army," Relan said.

She took the blade, hunger taking hold of her as her fingers wrapped around the hilt.

"If you go into the city you will be on your own. My mission is mine and mine alone, as is yours, do you understand?" he asked.

She nodded.

"Very well, shield maiden, until we meet again," he said.

With a wave of his hands the Druid's form shifted, the staff vanishing and where a man once stood a bird took flight, its small wings beating their way toward the distant castle.

Hunger burned inside her, the blade pulling her on as she slowly started to run, the city coming closer and closer with each step.

Hovering in the air, the brown thrush shimmered and changed form. Relan appeared before the main gate of Lystbrook castle, his staff still held before him.

No guard stood at the portcullis, the great gate open and dry leaves playing in the courtyard beyond. He stepped over the threshold, the twin inner keeps playing out to either side. The queen's was a collection of white stone that spilled down to a secluded cove at the far end of the bay, and the king's was a grey set of towers, walls, and gates that surrounded the bulk of the hill.

He strode through the main courtyard, the doors of a mighty stable left open with a smithy sitting cold and dark beyond it. A set of steps led up from the yard into gardens, and beyond was another rising stair that wound up the hill to the tower keep where the top parapets still flew the colors of the kingfisher on a blue field.

He moved up into the tower keep, his boots echoing on the stone. The sound of the surf far below drifted up the stair, echoed from the stone of the tower as the wind moaned through arches and open windows.

The King is here, and there is a taint is in his element: the kiss of my master's former lover, the goddess of suffering.

Light shown from the tip of his staff as a tendril of energy went swirling away up the tower stairs and out of sight.

You sense him too, I see, then we shall find him together.

The magic of his staff lead him further and further up the twisting steps until the outer stair entered an open portal to the tower's interior. Tapestries hung on the curved walls, and old weapons decorated archways. Heavy, carved wooden furniture sat in the entry and a stone stair led further up beyond an unmanned guard station.

He walked the steps, staff raised and his boots shuffling against the stone. The stair moved ever up, and his breath grew raspy as he ascended the final flight. Wind from somewhere above whipped at his hood as he entered the top chamber of the tower, his eyes finding only an empty room with a wooden stair leading to the observation turret above. He crossed the distance to the stair and gently pressed his boots onto the steps, as morning light streamed down from the opening. His staff warmed in his hand and he took each step slowly, the firebirds leading the way.

Be wary, old friend, I can smell the stink even with the wind swirling above.

He rose onto the platform, the sea spanning three quarters of the view around him. The height gave him an instant feeling of vertigo, while the howl of the wind and calls of the gulls rose up from hundreds of feet below his position.

A lone figure stood at the parapet, the man's eyes ruddy amber, and his silken robes flapping wildly in the wind. A golden kingfisher was embroidered over his heart, and he clutched an etched broadsword in one bejeweled fist.

"King Ergoroth?" Relan called over cry of the wind.

The man tilted his head slightly but made no reply.

"I've come to set things in balance. I am Relan of the Druids Council, Warden of the North and walker of the woodland realms," Relan continued.

The king tilted his head in the opposite direction, his fire spark alight and its taint leaving a bad taste in Relan's mouth.

"I was called by my Maker, the Oak Father, to halt the destruction of the Wintertide by an army from Lystbrook, an army led by your own son."

At this the king croaked a single word, "Wilam?"

Relan pulled his staff close, saying, "As was my godly duty, I laid your son's host low and buried them under a blanket of snow so thick not one of them could have survived."

"Wilam..." the king said again.

"Dead," Relan replied.

A scream tore from the man's throat and heat bloomed upon the distance between them.

Watch yourself, he's found the link to his spark.

The king raised his blade and charged, but Relan stepped away from the stair and brought his staff forward. The firebirds bloomed, but the king simply charged into their heat and slashed the staff from his path with a single heavy blow.

Relan adjusted, and the king swung again, but this time the staff, now held in two hands, blocked the strike. Along the edge of the king's blade, a sheen of scarlet appeared, waves of heat coming off it as he pulled away and screamed once more.

Wind tore at their cloaks, and they exchanged several blows as they moved about the height.

He is mad and has no care for safety in his person.

Another powerful strike from the king hammered the staff, and the energy from the blow sapped strength from Relan's arms. Stepping back, the druid took the staff in his left hand and pressed – palm out – with his right at the king.

Air swirled around him and struck his opponent like a physical blow, the king's feet sliding across the wooden planks as he cut at the air with is blade.

Keep him back and off balance.

The king screamed and renewed his charge, but Relan threw his palm forward again, the king's course halted as another blast of wind drove him back.

Heat cascaded from the tower's top, the wood around the king's feet smoking where his boots touched, and beads of sweet breaking out on Relan's forehead.

Use his madness and power against him.

Another charge, and Relan let the king come within eight feet before he struck him again with the air burst, causing rage to seethe from the king's cracked lips as he slid back across the floor. Relan took a step back, the parapet close behind him where he let his staff falter, putting his hand to his head to steady his vision.

The king jumped, running at full speed with sword raised high. His boots hammered the planks as he charged, and Relan took another, staggered step back, then executed his feint with a quick sidestep as the king drew close enough to swing.

Raising his palm he ducked beneath the lethal swing, came up behind the king and struck him with another air burst in the back. The force of the air broke the king's frantic halt and lifted him up and over the lip of the parapet.

The man screamed like a banshee as he fell, and Relan walked slowly to the edge of the tower, watching impassively as the final curse was broken on the rocks below.

"This house is at an end," Relan whispered.

From his vantage, he saw the small frame of the king broken on the rocks far below, and looking up to the sea he made out a dark outline on the water beyond the ringed arms of Sastrine Bay. The shape of a single ship moved steadily across the blue waves. Near fifty oars struck in unison against the smooth surface as the boat pulled toward the shore.

Is this what you were waiting for up here?

"Far too near,
Like the eagle seeking the prairie hare,
I ask to see."

The focus of his eyes moved to the ship as though his body flew across the water, the distance brought near in the eagle's line of his vision.

The ship was dark, and men in boiled leather and pointed helms pulled against the oars of the longboat as it cut the waves. On the aft of the vessel a man in half-plate and tabard watched the distant bay coming closer and closer with each pull.

Relan studied the tabard, its triple starburst of gold embroidered on a scarlet field.

Arcania! The merchant princes and the ladies of suffering have a hand in this.

Frowning, he cast his sight further out to sea, his enhanced vision pulling the seascape to him for miles. Out on the open ocean a great fleet plied the water, their dark hulls and crimson-and-gold banners marking them as more Arcanian mercenary vessels.

The ships were on the move, their sails full as the stormy trades pulled them ever southward toward the shallow Caliper Inlets and the coast of distant Aflyr.

My master's dark mistress, goddess or no, has made her play for Lystbrook and now she's after Aflyr. Perhaps she feels if she controls both lands she will force their son into the light and can bring him to her bosom just as Belmarillian feared.

Turning his eyes back to the longboat, he spoke again to the Oak Father, the words of power immediately ripped away by the wind.

"Seas will rise and fall,
Turning waters spin and suck,
As the waves take into them what they will."

As he watched, the smooth sea around the longboat began to churn. The waves turned white, and the men began to shout as the water turned the boat away from the shore. The captain on the aft cried out for order, but as the ocean licked the sides of the ship, a panic spread. The darkness beneath the boat grew and madness struck the oarsmen as sailors tried to jump free of the developing vortex. The swirling ocean pulled each mercenary down as they leapt off the ship, while timbers groaned and cracked amidships, spilling more doomed souls into the darkness. In a matter of minutes, the sea claimed the boat, the oars, and every last man sent to pillage and claim the city of Sastrine.

When the water was again still, Relan turned from the tower and let the eagle vision fade from his eyes.

The black fleet is too far for my powers now, but I know a place they must pass close if they are making for Mahe.

Walking from the tower's roof, he made haste toward the castle gates, clouds now running in from the east and a chill in the air.

CHAPTER FOUR

ERIK

So she was close, so close I could almost taste her, and then some ridiculous god's meddling had to come in and blow the whole thing apart.

No disrespect, but I really hate the gods even if I worship one when the occasion presents itself. They always seem to have an agenda, and they certainly love to use mortals to play their games.

I'm sure more lives than an Aspara Sage could count have been lost to their interference, and yet we keep right on feeding their temples and providing them young worshipers.

Ah well, that isn't really within my power to resolve at the moment. My time is better spent trying to survive as this bloody war breaks out around me. What I'm doing at the center of it is beyond me, although I'm pretty sure it has to do with Igrayn, and that in itself stinks of the meddling of gods.

Outriders pulled up short, both men's cheeks flared red and their breath coming in white plumes from both horse and rider.

"Tall Hills looks to be clear, and the pass was still open when we left it yesterday morning," a scout said.

Erik adjusted his position in his saddle and craned his neck to look back at the men still coming up the trail behind him. They were five hundred strong, helms glittering in the morning sun and lances adorned with banners that fluttered in the breeze.

"Good work! Find fresh horses with the quartermaster and take provisions where you can," Erik ordered.

The riders saluted and road past, Malcolm moving up to ride beside him, saying, "We have at least two more days headed east before we make Tall Hills pass, but the men are in good spirits and the supplies we gathered at Seahollow have provisioned us for another week at least. It looks like luck is on our side."

"Unless we find snow along the road over the inlands. We can't control the weather and it's very late in the season," Braxus offered.

Erik nodded. Further back he could hear Ash telling the story of Bandylegs and the Delver Demon Chief's duel on the planar isle of Pandemonium.

Looking back he saw Tavalori riding with the Eldaryn, and something about the woodsman's expression reminding him of Raziel.

Where is that bodyguard? When we left the cursed palace he'd fled the Temple of the Sun and killed a priest in the process.

"A standard bearer," Lieutenant Rikov said from his right.

The Lieutenant was a lean fellow, blonde-bearded and long nosed, and Erik nodded to him before following the man's outstretched arm.

On the road a single armored figure moved from the rocks and skeletal trees. The stocky newcomer carried a russet flag flapping in the fall breeze, its colors broken in twain by a black axe painted along the diagonal.

"Kin," Malcolm said.

The Freeaxe Prides. I've seen that banner in the hall of my father since I was a boy, but I've never met one of the Kin whom it represents.

Spurring SmokeShadow forward, Erik made his way to the waiting Kin before pulling up short and dropping from the saddle.

The standard bearer was lightly onyx-skinned, with grey veins like marble running along her exposed flesh, for upon closer examination she was certainly female. A tangle of green moss began at an indentation at her skull and flowed down her back. Armor adorned a chest plated around two large breasts, and a hammer the size of a human's leg rested on a thong about her shoulders.

"Greetings Stone Mistress," Erik bowed.

The Kin was near four and a half feet in height, and as he bowed to her their eyes met, a collection of facets in her brown irises looking like cut gems.

"Hail rider. I speak for those under of the mountain," the Kin replied.

Erik nodded, "What message do you bring?"

"Delvers slip from the Broken Land," the Kin replied. "The Blood Skins have slipped over the eastern border of Araba'Duur and are now in Aflyr."

"So we've seen. My cavalry have pressed them hard this side of the Yule," Erik said.

"Then Aflyr has gone to war with the Broken Land?" the Kin asked.

"So it would seem."

The Kin nodded and waved the banner high in the air. Erik turned back to his cavalry and waved them to stay, Malcolm and Braxus both a dozen feet ahead of the main column already.

"Our Sire will want to speak with you, but his pavilion is up on the meadows beyond the rocks and the road. Will you come?" she asked.

Erik nodded, "I would be honored to speak with the Kin Sire."

Around the rocks, more female Kin appeared, their bodies similarly armored and the smell of earth powerful about them.

"Then follow, and we will see you safely to him," she said.

Erik gave a final wave to this column and motioned Malcolm and Braxus to set camp. The two nodded, and he followed the dozen Kin women up into the heights, the heavy-shouldered warriors nimble as mountain goats among the rocks.

A light snow had begun to fall by the time he made the high pasture, a collection of no less than a hundred female Kin nesting among the rocks with short blades, hand axes, hammers, and picks.

He made his way through the winter wheat, a pavilion of dark canvas and stone having been laid out near the western wall of the meadow and the mountains shielding it on three sides. The structure was carved with scrollwork that cut the stone in exacting detail, some script or story playing out in it from front to back.

"The Sire is waiting," his guide said.

Nodding, he entered past the flap on the pavilion as heat washed over him. The interior was just as magnificent at its walls, the inside having been lined with snow wolf furs and mithril shields depicting the various Kin Prides of Araba'Duur. Silver lamps hung from dark wooden supports casting light on the Sire's shining suit of plate that now hung on a cross of wood near a stout chair. Both were gilded in gold.

Hearty beer had been brought out and placed in silver tankards that sat before thick cushions made from Arcanian silk, and the smell of deep earth and fragrant jasmine hung in the air.

Upon the throne a mighty Kin sat, his body black and the mineral-like veins in his skin glimmering of gold. He was broad-shouldered, bow-legged, and no moss mane adorned his great, hairless, and bat-winged head.

"Have a seat, young knight, as it is my boon to show you the same respect and courtesy as you would find from any of your own kings in the lands of humanity," he said.

His voice was thick and hearty, the rumble of it felt in Erik's chest as he stood before him.

"I thank you for your kind service," Erik bowed.

Nodding, the Sire took up one of the great tankards and directed Erik to the other, saying, "Let us toast to the felling of Delvers and the sudden renewal of old alliances."

Erik lifted the tankard, the weight daunting as he brought it to his lips. The beer within was rich and bold, the flavor mixed with foreign spices that burned his nose and forced a belch from his throat.

The Sire laughed, a ring of white suds about his dark lips.

"Our brew is not for all, but once you acquire a taste there is little else you will desire in this world," the Sire said.

"It does have some girth," Erik replied.

The Sire nodded before taking another drink.

"You have come with a small army, a princess and a Wizard, if my spies are correct," the Sire said.

"That's true."

"And why would you risk such prizes, especially the noble womb, when an alliance between Aflyr and Lystbrook hangs upon her safe delivery?" the Sire asked.

Alliance? What is he talking about?

"I'm not sure I understand," Erik said.

The Sire regarded him with gold-flecked brown eyes, corded muscles beneath the skin in his chest flexing. He was primal, half-again larger than the females, and danger lurked within his alien face.

"Does a Knight of Aflyr not understand what he's protecting?" the Sire asked.

"I'm afraid you have me at a loss, Sire," Erik said.

The Sire took a long drink, laid down this tankard and then leaned forward, saying, "Igrayn Ergoroth, your princess, is to marry the NyWinter King of Aflyr come spring, and if she's not delivered intact there will be war, or so I would think."

Igrayn is to marry? Then why is she here? Why would Lystbrook risk her, and again, what game was Raziel playing as her protector?

"I was not aware of this," Erik said.

"Then you are now, and I suggest you send that girl away before whatever alliance we strike here today is put in jeopardy by her death," the Sire said.

Erik nodded, "If I had the power I would do so, but she controls her own destiny and has determined to go to Nehru as a champion of these people."

The Sire smiled, "Fierce is she, like the women of the Kin? Well, I have warned you nonetheless, and when your King finds out what you have done I would hold tight that knighthood because it will certainly be stripped from you."

"I'm no Knight of the NyWinter King, I serve the people of Mahe," Erik said.

Sitting back in his throne, the Sire regarded him a long moment then said, "There hasn't been a true Knight of Mahe in a thousand years."

"Well, there is now, and I will hold only to the people of that city to judge what I have done, and they hold no love of either Lystbrook or the NyWinter King who abandoned them to the Delvers sweeping across the land."

Erik's spark was alight and he took another drink of the beer, the liquid churning his stomach.

"I see great pride in you, Human, but there is nobility there as well. So be it, if you speak for Mahe and the West, then I will treat with you. Shall we talk of alliance?" the Sire asked.

Erik nodded, the Sire calling for more Kin women to enter and bring the materials for a treaty.

Now I've done it, spoken for the Cursed Legion and the West. Still, it's the thought of Igrayn betrothed that brings bile to my throat. That, is news I hadn't expected, and Bandylegs and his meddling play directly into the story.

Erik strode about the command tent of his company, Malcolm, Braxus, and Lieutenant Rikov standing as he paced before them.

"Sire Freeaxe says that Nehru has been besieged, that the great eastern wall has been destroyed by Jai-Ruk earth breakers and that the West Keep now stands as a lone island amid a siege that surrounds it. However, the bulk of a massive Delver army has now slipped into the east, as a rear guard set about finishing what remains," Erik said.

"Fell news, commander," Rikov said.

"How many are left to the siege?" Malcolm asked.

"Two thousand Delvers, and a tenth of that in Jai-Ruk commanders," Erik answered.

"We could never take so many, especially in the mountains where their earth magic is the strongest," Rikov stated.

A sentry pulled open the flap, a wool scarf wrapped around his helm and his riding blanket draped over his bronze plate.

"Commander, the hillmen have arrived and Cronin wants to speak to you," he said.

"How many?" Rikov asked.

"Near a thousand if my eyes are right."

Erik looked to his commanders, each raising eyebrows.

"I guess Cronin delivers when he promises 'support,'" Braxus said.

"Show Cronin up here to the tent, and see to his men if you can, but I suspect they'll be self-supporting if they got this far," Erik said.

The sentry saluted and left, Rikov the first to speak, "Even with a thousand hillmen, we're no match for Delvers and Jai-Ruks in their own element."

"Don't forget about the west keep. There will still be knights and soldiers there," Braxus said.

"True, but if they've been under siege more than a month, they'll be mostly spent when a battle comes," Malcolm said.

"Then I guess it's a good thing I signed an alliance between Mahe and Araba'Duur," Erik said.

All three of his subordinates started at him.

"It's true, and don't ask me what it costs, all that matters is there will be Kin with us, and there's no higher earth element in the Nameless Realms than the Kin," Eric continued.

"How many will come?" Rikov asked.

"Sire Freeaxe has pledged his Pride of more than a hundred females, and three other Prides with half that number each," Erik answered.

"Two-hundred and fifty Kin and four Sires...that's a substantial force," Malcolm observed.

"There's also a good chance more rogue Sires will join as we march. He has dozens of sons that lurk along the mountain roads, as do the other Pride Sires. Once they get a whiff of so many females on the move and battle at hand, they'll come out to test their strength and try to claim a pride of their own," Erik said.

"So we now have an army, cavalry, foot, and Kin, but we've still got to make the Tall Hills pass or none of that will matter," Braxus said.

"Agreed," Erik began. "Braxus, you spread the word among the men. On the morrow we're marching hard to Nehru with the hillmen and the Kin at our side," Erik said.

Braxus nodded and left the tent, Rikov moving to the flap as well, "I'll see to the horses, make sure they're ready as well."

Erik nodded, and the Lieutenant left, only Malcolm remaining.

"What say you?" Erik asked.

"Your rise is unmatched even in any legends I was told as a child. A month ago you were a half-broke sellsword and today you're negotiating treaties for Western Aflyr."

"It does seem like a pretty dramatic reversals of fortune, I'll agree."

Malcolm nodded, "But you take to it, and the more I watch you do it the more I know there is a story behind you that we've not heard."

Erik smiled, "Every man has a story."

"True, and I'll leave you to yours," Malcolm said before he left the tent as well.

I guess my story is still being written, and I pray it has some part of a happy ending.

CHAPTER FIVE

SAFFRON AND RELAN

I run. I run for my life and I run for the lives of my people, the city becoming a blur around me as I make for the only home I can truly remember.

The Druid says the King is there, my foster father, and that he will kill him. I cannot stop that, not with these mundane legs, so all I can do is keep running and hope that there is something, anything, left to save once I get there.

As a shield maiden I have protected nothing, only myself, and in my hand a possessed sword ravages my thoughts with hungry lusts. I have to wonder what has become of me, what purpose I now serve since I have failed so wholly in my former duties.

So I run, and only the lonely streets are left to witness my passing.

Saffron slowed, her breath coming in great puffs and her legs burning beneath her britches. Around her the familiar ring of the smithy and the barking of dogs had been replaced with the sound of the wind. Cold, salt-tinged air forced its way into her lungs as she pressed on toward the gate which stood open and abandoned like everything else.

Retracing the steps she had taken while on horseback only a week before, she passed the empty stables and then the staircases that led to the keep proper. Her climb was checked by the howling wind. A storm was brewing on the surface of the Halo, and its call sent breakers crashing against the Queen's retreat below.

She found a servant's entry to the King's Keep and slipped out of the wind. The air inside was warmer but her breath still came out in a white mist, and she kept her hooded cloak down over her face.

Her footfalls echoed on the hewn-stone floors polished by years of servant's shoes that had worn the hill granite down to a bowed surface. She made her way inward through several connecting rooms, and then upward along the back stair of the grand meeting hall. As stealthily as a thief, she slipped between two hand-carved pillars to the right of the King's throne where the Castilian normally stood.

The distinct smell of cherry smoke drifted to her nostrils and she eased her heeled boots along the stone to conceal her passage until she had a better view of the full extent of the chamber.

Banners still hung along the walls, with the chairs of state standing at attention before the throne as if expecting petitioners to enter any moment for case review.

It's a ruse. The heart has left this court, and all that remains is an empty shell.

She moved along the line of pillars until at last she could glimpse the great fireplace that had been crafted by Kin masons from Arcania. It dated from when Sarah the First still ruled beneath the vaults of the ancient chamber.

Kneeling before the smoking and cracking fire was a solitary figure, his shoulders slumped and his head bowed in prayer. At his hip the gold-leaf hilt of a sword protruded from his winter cloak. She inhaled sharply.

Wilam.

The sound of her shock drifted through the vault, and Wilam turned like a viper, a black-fingered hand falling to his blade. She staggered back, his eyes blazing as he looked upon her. He was a ruin, his nose having fallen away, eyes sunken, fingers black, and ears little more than nubs of dark flesh.

"Saffron!" he hissed.

Relan had walked through the growing gloom of evening, his boots crunching the frost that clung to the undergrowth of the Wintertide.

I've come so far and yet the boy, Tavalori, is still a distant dream, but if he is to remain outside my providence then so too shall he be beyond hers.

Stopping, he looked around the small, snow-covered clearing he'd entered and smiled. Reaching inside his robes, he withdrew a tiny seed and knelt to the frozen earth in the middle of the clearing.

With both hands he drove the shaft of his staff into the earth, the heat from it melting away the white powder and turning the frozen dirt below into mud. He left the staff in place several minutes before withdrawing it and placing the seed in the vacated hole.

Taking a seat on the damp earth, he placed his staff across his folded legs and closed his eyes.

"Seasons change and time slips,
Let the moons and suns pass,
Allow this seed to grow out of the flow."

Opening his eyes, he watched the ground as a small green shoot sprang forth and wound its way upward. Slowly, leaves unfolded and stretched from the base of a delicate plant. In another five minutes the greenery began flowering in the chilly air of the settling winter night.

Holding his staff aloft, the firebirds glowed, the plant was illuminated in a golden glow. The deep green leaves were covered with droplets of water and small flowers bloomed about them. Raising his fist, he prayed again.

"Workers come and collect,
Like you do in the spring,
When your queen calls you to muster."

He opened his palm and half a dozen bees appeared. They flew from his outstretched fingers and buzzed about the flowers until their legs were covered with golden pollen.

More minutes passed, the flowers turning and dying, but, behind the buds, fruit swelled and turned bright scarlet. Sweet strawberries the size of an Eldaryn's fist grew along the leaves making them fall low to the frosty ground.

Sensing the ebb in his spell, Relan let the magic fade and waved away the insects that disappeared as suddenly as they had come, only puffs of yellow pollen marking where they had been flying in the air around the plant.

Extinguishing the light of his staff, he plunged the clearing into moonlit shadow, the Ghost Moon looming high above the skeletal trees.

He waved a hand, wind sweeping around him carrying with it the sweet smell of the ripened fruit.

The moon had moved only slightly in its path across the starlit sky when the first light appeared in the trees around the clearing. The tiny glow danced and snaked through the trunks for a moment before another appeared and then another.

A dozen sparks now tested the breeze, the light closing in around the strawberry plant. Relan watched quietly as little winged figures within the glow came to life around him.

"Strawberries!" a rose-colored fairy exclaimed, her glow lighting a large fruit almost as big as her tiny body.

"It is too late in the season for something like this," a green male said.

Relan made no motion as he watched them buzz around him and the plant.

Fairies are odd creatures, always far too focused on what they want than what lies around them.

"How sweet they must be," another male commented.

"But how?" an amber female asked.

"A gift from the Oak Father," the male answered.

"In a way," Relan said.

At the sound of his voice, the lights scattered, fleeing away into the gloom like little balls of lightning.

Relan waited a moment, then spoke, "I've summoned the fruit for you in payment for a service."

The trees were dark for a minute before the light reappeared from behind them, the little creatures looking from their hiding places.

"What do you want of us, Forest Master?" a male shouted, his tiny voice like music from the tree line.

"He is cute," a female voice whispered from another tree.

Relan shook his head, answering, "I have come seeking passage to the point of rocks in the sea several days travel from this spot. Do you know it?"

Silence followed, punctuated now and then by whispers.

"The place where the sea crashes all around?" the male asked.

Relan nodded his head. "Yes."

"We know it, but the price is too high for simple fruit," the male said.

Relan sighed, "Very well, then I shall have of this fruit and be gone."

Raising a hand, he reached out to take a strawberry.

"Wait!" several voices screamed in unison.

Relan raised an eyebrow. "Yes?"

Many lights now danced from the trees, twice as many as he had seen before.

"We will do as you ask, just leave the fruit. The winter will be long, and we do so love spring sweets," the little amber female said as she flew up to illuminate his face in the moonlight.

"It is a fair bargain then." Relan said, the little lights dancing around the clearing over the ice-covered snow, their reflection glimmering over the surface like they were dancing on glass.

The fairies collected in a great circle, their wind playing with the snow as they whispered and danced in the air. The little creatures sang and prayed using magic gifted to them by the Oak Father during their creation in ages past. It was an older magic than Relan's, but familiar. He could almost understand the words if he focused on them. Beneath their reverie, the snow trembled, and, from within it, dark shoots slithered and twisted until their heads burst open in a crowning cap.

Toadstools, a great ring of them, found their way through the snow into the light of the moon. All the while the fairies continued their dance with glee. Beside Relan, the amber female appeared and snuck a kiss on his cheek.

"The circle awaits you, Forest Master," she giggled flying before his eyes.

Nodding at her, he got to his feet and collected his things. She danced around him as he moved to the circle, his boots stepping over the line of fungus and crunching into the snow as he took his place in the center of the circle.

He was about to thank the creatures when the wind howled and the salt air sprayed his cheeks. Around him the world had changed.

Instead of the frozen Wintertide thickets, he found himself in a copse of pine with jagged and broken rocks behind him catching the crashing waves of the Caliper Straits.

Relan shook his head.

That was faster than I expected.

Finding his bearings, he turned to the jutting rocks of the point and made his way south, his boots sometimes sliding on the salt-slick boulders that made the pinnacle of land.

Soon the sun will rise on another day, and the dark fleet will move into view. When they do, I will strike a blow for the Council, and let the dark mistress rage from the far side of the sea.

Hunger.

Saffron's blade jumped to her hand before Wilam had made half the distance to her. She felt and heard the desire within the blade echoed from her own soul, a wave of passionate need bringing saliva to her lips.

"You will be a final prize for me," Wilam spat.

His steps were leaden, and drool fell from broken lips, but his heat washed over her like an inferno.

The runes on her sword flashed as she brought the blade up before her eyes in a quiet salute to her half-brother. He stopped short, his mad eyes flicking from the blade to her and back again.

"Where did you get that?" he hissed.

She was about to reply when he struck, the strength in his arms twice that of her own. The sudden assault sent sparks skittering across the floor as she turned his attack to the side. With a quick stride, she danced back behind a pillar.

Wilam struck again, his mad desire to see her dead driving him around the pillar and forcing her back out into the open. Her boots played and scraped across the stone hall as she parried each cleaving blow. He was using all his insane strength against her, each blow over-handed and meant to deal death in a single strike.

If this was practice I'd let him wear himself out, but I've no points to allow here and one false move means I'm dead.

Another blow struck, and her arms ached, but she managed to dance behind a chair and call out, "What do you know!?"

He struck her again, this time bringing his weight into the blow so much that she felt a pain rack her left shoulder as she absorbed the impact.

She winced and leapt away, her boots carrying her to the fireplace until she could feel the heat at her back and Wilam's elemental fire on her face.

"From what hall of my family have you stolen *Soif De Sang*, thief?" he demanded.

Soif De Sang… now I know your name!

"Queen Sarah gave the blade to me," she called back.

Wilam froze for a moment before he again brought his blade forward and struck at her. This time she was ready, and with a deft parry followed by a back-cut she scored a slice of dark red along Wilam's right leg.

He didn't even wince, but as his blood was tasted by her blade, the runes blazed amber along the length. Strength pulsed into her arm, and she smiled.

Swinging his sword like a smith tempering iron, Wilam clashed again and again against her defense as she used the size of the room to her advantage stepping away with each blow in a slow circle. Soon, his heavy boots grew slow, and her own feet played light as she cut him again with the blade.

Soif De Sang drank again, and the runes now glowed so brightly they showered the room in their glow. Saffron watched closely as the rage inside Wilam dwindled as the sword's light waxed stronger, whatever strength drove him finally fading.

He paused, sucking for breath through his mouth and ruined nose. She sprang at him, surprised as he again deflected her attacks with his wider blade.

With eyes flashing and his strength gone, Wilam again spoke.

"With me gone, then the whole of Lystbrook is gone as well. I am the last of my line."

She smirked at that, her blade dancing around his as it took another drink from his right arm.

He cursed and spun away, his boots taking him once again to the fire.

"Igrayn is safe from you, no matter what you've done to your mother and father," Saffron replied.

Wilam returned her smirk with a wicked grin of his own, saying, "Don't be so certain, little girl, as my man was to kill her once they reached the Aflyrian border."

Saffron froze, the words ringing in her mind.

Fool, I knew it was a trap and yet I kept my tongue.

Bringing his sword up hard, he moved *Soif De Sang* away enough that he could force his body close. With an impact like that of a bull, the prince shouldered her up and into the air, her lungs blasted free of breath.

Like a man without reason he leapt forward again, his blade raised above his head. Her eyes saw white stars as she tried to right herself, *Soif De Sang* heavy in her grasp as the shadow of Wilam appeared in the air above her.

A scream of intense pain burst from her lips as Wilam's blade pierced her chest and sunk into the stone floor beneath her nearly to the hilt. Darkness fought against light, her grievous wound only checked by her own blade, *Soif De Sang* having found home in Wilam's gut when he leapt atop her.

Sarah's cursed blade drank fresh blood and channeled the energy back into her body.

Looking up, she saw the clouded and dead eyes of Wilam as he drooled on her, his body supported by her blade's guard, mere inches from her own chest. Closing her eyes, she tried to regain focus.

I've got to move. Once his blood ebbs so will the restorative magic and I'll die like a butterfly pinned to a lady's summer collection.

Opening her eyes, she looked to the side and then turned her wrist so that *Soif De Sang* fell away from her, taking the heavy body of Wilam with it. The action freed her from the threat above, but the twisting motion nearly snapped her wrist as she clung to the hilt of her sword for dear life.

Her breathing became fevered as she turned back to stare at the blade wedged through her lower ribs. The hilt was perhaps four inches above her flesh and after a tentative movement she knew she would never be able to withdraw it from the stone beneath.

Laying her head back on the stone she stared at the ceiling and considered any option left to her. *Soif De Sang* still blazed and pulsed beside her, but the now white corpse of her half-brother was nearly drained.

Gods, help me find the strength.

Biting deeply into her lower lip, she put her left hand on the hilt of Wilam's blade and pushed with all her might. The blade stayed in place, but the magically enchanted edge cut through her abdomen as she screamed out a ghastly wail.

Blood covered the floor and her head swam as she rolled away, both her hands grasping the hilt of *Soif De Sang* as it drew the last of Wilam's element from his body and transferred it to the huge gash in her abdomen.

She wept, shook, and finally lay still. Her fingers were numb, and her mouth dry as the pain started to fade. Darkness played at the corners of her vision and she uttered several curses.

I've got to fight. I can't let this end me, not here, not like this.

Pushing the prince's body over, she dragged *Soif De Sang* up and placed its pulsing tip against the thick wool of his tunic. Her breath coming in shallow rasps, she pushed with all the strength she had left, the blade moving in, glancing against a rib and then finding his heart.

Runes once again sprang to life on the blade and her eyes flew wide as she sucked in a deep gulp of air.

Pain registered and she screamed once more, but it faded quickly and she lay panting next to the shriveled corpse.

Drawing her forehead against the flat of her sword she whispered, "I'll not forget the gift you've given me this day."

Only silence and the popping of the fire gave reply, but no feeling of hunger passed into her. The blade was finally sated.

After many long minutes, she regained her feet and moved slowly to the fire. There, she sat and warmed her hands and feet as the blood turned brown on her clothing.

Igrayn. If you are alive, by some strange hand of fate, I'll find you. There is nothing left for me here.

The fire continued to burn and she slipped finally into a long and fitful sleep.

CHAPTER SIX

ERIK

Is it wrong that a part of me wishes for snow? Is there a soul out there that truly wants to be in battle? I've faced the Trench of Skulls and lived to tell the tale, but the terror and then deadly calm that takes over when a melee begins isn't something I'd wish for anyone I loved, or any kind soul for that matter.

So here I am, leading this army across a frozen mountain and wishing that the sky would open and keep us from the clash of steel that waits beyond.

It's either wish for that or sit on this horse and dream dark dreams about Igrayn and the King NyWinter. I'm a fool, but you know this don't you? The more I think about him having her, the more I want her myself. Spoiled to the core, that's what my handmaid used to say, and she was right as much as it stings me to admit it.

Shera saw something else inside me, probably whatever it is that keeps this army moving and following me, but there are times in the quiet when my demons rise and I can't help but listen to them...

It took them a full day to march up the eastern hills while early winter snow continued to fall intermittently. The light powder covered the dry hills with stark, white sheets that blew in the night wind and chilled men to the bone.

Erik rode in the late afternoon, the Kin vanguard and Sire Freeaxe had fallen back and Erik watched the pass rise up in twin bastions of rock on either side of the trail. Behind him hooves sounded and he turned to see Telluria urging her mount forward.

You've kept your distance these past weeks, so why do you come forward now?

The smell of the ocean came with her, foreign among these inland heights and the spark in his chest guttered as she drew up next to him.

"Erik," she said.

"Telluria," he replied.

"Malcolm says there will be a battle on the far side of the pass?" she asked.

"Yes, there is a small force there, only a couple hundred, but they hold a fortified position so the cavalry will be useless and we'll have to really on or strength in the melee," he said.

"If they have a defensive work, I should be able to disrupt it," she said.

He turned to her. She wore a white cloak trimmed in gold, a fur hood drawn up around her head exposing just her face, allowing several long lengths of slick black hair that shimmered green near the tips to fall out. The staff of the Lich Elim lay across her saddle, twin blades framing the head of it like an axe, and runes cut into its dark surface from tip to tip.

"Has the staff given you such power?" Erik asked.

She smiled, her face flawless, pale, and lovely. "The staff holds a great reservoir of the *Afterglow*, but I've also grown in power since you saved me from the Delvers in the fens."

"Is that why you've taken the white and gold?" he asked.

"Yes, I'm no longer an apprentice to the Order, and I've chosen a path of defense as my realm of study. Thus the white and gold I now wear," she answered.

"And Elim's garb of black and gold?" he asked.

"Necromancy and the study of the shadow plane," she replied.

"You speak of a world I don't understand," he said.

"Few do, and fewer still have travelled with one of our number in their company," she said.

"Then I should consider myself lucky."

She reached up and tucked a bit of hair behind her ear with a white-gloved hand, her emerald eyes going to the road ahead. They rode a few minutes in silence before he spoke again, "You're close to Igrayn?"

"Yes."

"Has she confided at all in the contract that binds her to Aflyr?" he asked.

"How do you know of that contract?" she asked.

The smell of the ocean increased, and he pulled his horse a step away from her as she turned to stare at him.

"The Kin Sire knew of it and he asked why she was here putting herself in jeopardy when the fate of two nations rested on her being delivered safe to King NyWinter in the spring," he answered.

"She has not spoken of it to me," Telluria said. "But I do know of the contract as my former master was the one who drew up the document and saw it placed in the Order archives."

"The Order drafted the contract?"

"Yes, we are a neutral third party with the power to enforce the letter of the law. The Order often brokers such deals between nations when neither side trusts one another."

"Then the Order will see the contract fulfilled?"

"Yes."

He turned back to the road eyes narrow and teeth chewing on his bottom lip.

"NyWinter will have her then, and there's nothing I can do about it..." he muttered.

"No, the King of Aflyr will have her, the contract states nothing about King NyWinter," Telluria replied.

"What?" Erik asked.

Telluria stared forward, her face emotionless, "The contract states that Igrayn Ergoroth, princess of Lystbrook, is to marry the King of Aflyr. Faust NyWinter was near forty winters when the contract was drafted nearly two decades ago, and to ensure that the contract bound the two kingdoms he worded it as such so that his heir, Prince Arol, would marry the princess if Faust himself passed on before the contract came to fruition."

Erik pulled up his horse, as did Telluria, the two of them staring at each other for a long moment.

"You shouldn't have done that," he said.

She tilted her head, the slightest hint of a smile on her lips, "What?"

"Do you know what I am?" he asked.

"I know what Tavalori is, I know that the gods play a game on the fields of Aflyr, and people will die one way or another. But to answer your question, no, I don't know what you are, but I have a feeling I know what you're capable of, and that is why I told you," she said.

"This is insane"

"Insanity is the bedfellow of genius," she replied, without a hint of mockery.

He turned to look at the horses now coming up the road and picked the white and sapphire cloak of Igrayn out from the rest of the riders.

Don't do it, don't fall into this trap. You still have a choice and you can run...

"But you won't," Telluria said.

He looked back at Telluria, the Wizard's face a unreadable mask.

Reading minds, that's a new one. And she's right, I probably won't...

Kin scouts had cleared the eastern lookouts of any Delver spies before sunrise and had already reported back by the time Erik's army passed the midpoint of the pass.

A three hundred strong Kin vanguard marched before the lancers, and behind them the hillmen brought up the rear.

Erik adjusted his helmet as SmokeShadow galloped in the three inches of snow that had fallen on them in the early morning hours. Flakes still scattered from the clouds, but the brunt of the storm was past. The steel-grey sky held the edge of gloom to the field. Beside him, Braxus was testing his shield by striking it with a gauntleted hand. The mercenary looked awake and alive, as the time of battle quickly approached.

"Sleep well?" Erik asked him.

Braxus shot him a smile, "Like a newborn." His hand fell to the hilt of his sword, "And you?"

Erik gave a laugh, mist rising from his mouth, "I would've preferred the bed of a lady, but I managed all right."

Braxus looked back to where Igrayn rode with Ash at her back. She was again armored for battle, her chain oiled and her winged helm frosted with white wisps of snow.

"Any lady in particular?" Braxus asked.

Erik shot him a dark look, "I couldn't say."

"Not to worry, I'll see you through this little battle, and the Nehru siege that follows. Afterward, you can grant me access to a fine knighthood while you enjoy anything you 'couldn't say' in those warm halls," Braxus laughed.

"Don't make promises you can't keep. I know your loyalty lies with Bandylegs," Erik said.

Braxus smiled and shrugged his plated shoulders, the Kin horns blowing at the front of the vanguard. Thunder rumbled up the pass as the Kin women struck weapons against shields, and the smell of the earth clogged Erik's nose and layered his tongue.

There was a great cheer as the force rushed forward, the ground shaking beneath their feet. Erik turned and Telluria rode up next to him, Malcolm close behind.

"Can you see the defense?" she asked.

Erik lifted himself in his stirrups, his vantage making out a low earthen wall that stretched the width of the pass and was covered in sharpened wooden poles.

"The wall is there, do you see it?" Erik asked.

Telluria stood up as well, her hood falling back and her staff raised in the air.

"Yes," she said.

Waving the staff before her, she closed her eyes and wove her free hand as a painter might manipulate a brush on canvas. From the field before the onrushing Kin a tiny light flared. Then the world exploded.

A shower of heavy debris and white fire bloomed, and then showered the field where the middle of the wall once stood. The Kin flowed through it unchecked.

"By all the Gods..." Braxus whispered.

The smell of the depths saturated the cavalry, their armor beading with vapor, and Erik felt his spark shudder in his chest.

Telluria sat back on her mount, hair dripping water and her hood and shoulders dark with her native element.

"My reserves are gone, but I still have the staff for the coming conflict," Telluria said.

Erik shook his head.

What power. It is a wonder this race hasn't destroyed us all or chosen to rule the rest of the world's people like Gods on high.

Erik turned to his men and raised himself in the saddle so he could be heard over the din of the battle now raging up the pass.

"Today we cut the enemies' supply! Today we will see the blood of Delvers on our lances! Today we ride to victory!" he called to those behind him.

The knights cheered as they held their lances high. Erik swung back around and spurred SmokeShadow into a trot, the horse's hooves churning up the muddy ground. When he'd reached a hearty gait, he drew *Fury* from its scabbard and held it high in the air.

"Charge!" he screamed.

Driving SmokeShadow forward at full speed, he led the knights through the opening breach and crashed into the heart of the Delver camp. Low tents and smoldering cook fires were trampled in the charge as lances and blades struck down any scrambling Delvers who managed to avoid the horses' crushing hooves.

Fury danced back and forth over SmokeShadow's neck, Erik cutting down Delvers as they passed by. His men followed him and joined his battle rage, and together they refused to allow any attempt of Jai-Ruk commanders gain control of the field or form any type of rally point.

From Erik's flank Malcolm blew his cavalry horn and called his men to him. The lancers thundered into the rear of the east Delver pickets, driving the guardians back and breaking them in a single charge.

A scimitar swung up at Erik's face, but he turned it away and swung SmokeShadow around, brushing his assailant back as he fought to hold ground.

"Not today!" Braxus bellowed, bringing his sword down on the helm of the Jai-Ruk who had attacked Erik, the blade slitting both metal and skull in a single cleaving strike.

Erik nodded at the mercenary before spurring forward and taking another Jai-Ruk commander full in the chest with *Fury*. The force of the charge lifted the Ruk off his feet and cast him backward into his oncoming platoon. Erik quickly disengaged his blade, narrowly avoiding having it yanked from his grasp. The Delvers broke and ran, but the lancers coming behind made quick work of them.

Erik wheeled SmokeShadow about the field, another series of horns blowing from the pass. Sire FreeAxe led another charge from the main army as it poured into the open breach of the Delvers' defense, creating chaos among the gathering platoons to the north. About the Sire were a collection of rogue Sires, the male Kin having transformed to even more alien creatures and bashing away with great clubs, hammers, and spiked bars at anything in their path. The stink of their earth was so strong it nearly took his breath away.

With a smile Erik called to Braxus, and the two men lead another charge into a black company of Delvers mustering up to the south. The scuttling enemy was trying to organize a resistance on a low rise as their Jai-Ruk commander cursed and whipped at them with a cruel scourge.

CHAPTER SEVEN

ERIK

Watch it! I don't have time to entertain you obviously so just stay out of my head!

Another Ruk fell to *Fury*, and Erik spurred SmokeShadow over the rise as Malcolm's horn broke the din of battle.

The mercenary was surrounded, Delvers glowing with earthen power and his small collection of knights pulling back into a circle.

Where's Telluria?

"Braxus, find Telluria and get her to that fight!" Erik yelled.

Braxus road off at a full gallop and Erik charged on, twenty lancers behind him as he raced over the bloody field to the clash of arms around his friend.

Half way to the throng, two rogue Kin Sires appeared from the far side of a ditch beyond the combat and broke into the Delver flank with bar and hammer. The Delvers fell back, but the mass of them pulled three of Malcolm's company from their horses and another fired an arrow which lodged into Malcolm's right shoulder.

Go SmokeShadow, get me to his side!

Heat bloomed from Erik as he outpaced his company, several Delvers turning at his approach only to be cut down as he slammed into their platoon at full tilt. The stink of earth was overpowering, but he swung his blade right and left, his steed kicking and bucking as he turned round and round amid a gauntlet of dark spears.

An enemy caught him across the thigh and another fired an arrow in to his horse's flank, but his troop broke the Delver offensive and rallied around him with lance and sword spilling dark blood all over the mud.

Erik turned, Malcolm sagging in his saddle as blood streamed from beneath his dented helm. Only five of his lancers were still on horse, another two had drawn longswords and were back to back, swinging away from the ground.

There was a flash, and a swirling translucent lion of coalesced air leapt into the throng casting Delvers right and left with gargantuan claws. The smell of earth was blown away, as was the Delver's defense, even the Kin falling back as the air lion ripped through the platoon that temporarily blocked its path to Malcolm and his men.

Erik looked over his shoulder to see Telluria and Braxus riding hard toward the conflict, her staff held high and blood dripping from the blades at its head.

Good timing.

He swung *Fury* again, this time cleaving a fleeing Delver that made for the trench which had spawned the Kin. His men flanked him, and the fighting pitched for another five minutes before the men pulled up and the world returned to calm.

Beyond them, back at the earthen wall, Delvers, Ruks, Kin, and hillmen fought along the remaining length, but the tide was turned. The Delvers fell in great numbers as the alliance force swept them away with each new surge.

"We've broken them," Braxus said.

Erik looked for Malcolm. The mercenary was supported by one of his lancers, and Telluria was swiftly closing the distance.

"Yes, but how much have we lost in the process?"

Erik and SmokeShadow were both covered in gore by the time the Kin horns blew along the walls to signal the victory.

As the horns blared, he turned to the Braxus and tapped *Fury* against the side of his helm in a salute. Braxus repaid the courtesy with a gap-toothed smile and a scream of victory.

"Will each of our battles be greater than the last?" Braxus asked, turning on his horse and surveying the battlefield.

Erik looked around at the formation of Kin that began to break up to search for stragglers and dispatch any wounded enemy on the field.

"If they are, I hope we continue to remain on the winning side," Erik replied.

Braxus laughed, sliding from his horse and moving to the mangled body of a fallen Jai-Ruk. The mercenary knelt and removed a heavy cleaver from the dead warrior's hand. With several test swings, he smiled again and walked back to his horse.

"A trophy?" Erik asked.

"Another weapon for my arsenal," Braxus said.

If you can do half as much damage with that thing as a Ruk can, it will be a good choice.

"Sir Tall Hills!" called the now familiar bellow of Sire FreeAxe.

Erik turned from Braxus and found the Sire moving toward him with his honor guard in tow. All the Kin wives of the noble company were decorated with dark blood and other venerable scars of fresh battle. The Sire looked larger than he had even in his great chair, and the earth had changed him, making his face more alien still, and giving him an almost reptilian quality.

"The day is ours!" the Sire exclaimed.

Erik nodded, "Another victory for the annals of the Prides of Araba'Duur."

"Your southern border is now clear from Tall Hills to the sea, and if my scouts are correct, there's no further Delver presence all the way to Nehru Fortress," FreeAxe said.

"But I still have to wonder, all the Delvers we've encountered were scourge bands, nothing of a full army west of the Yule," Erik said thoughtfully

"And?" Freeaxe asked.

"And even with Mahe's defense in the hands of old men, it seems unlikely the bands even together could have taken the city by themselves."

Sliding from SmokeShadow's back, Erik flexed his legs and back as he returned *Fury* to its sheath.

The Sire frowned, saying, "Perhaps they wanted to bring their main force against ChanderNagor?"

"Perhaps, but I've a feeling Mahe might be under a threat we've yet to realize…"

"Would you return?" Freeaxe asked.

Erik shook his head, "No, we've come for Nehru, and if the Ruks and Delvers are on to the capital, then we can cut their supply if we retake the fortress. Besides, the Legion now rests in Mahe, and they should handle any unseen threat."

Erik turned back to Braxus, who was industriously trying to find a spot on his saddle for his new cleaver. Erik understood his difficulty. There was not a single spot on the worn leather that did not already have a deadly implement attached to it.

"Find Malcolm and Telluria. I need to know if he's survived. I'll take fifteen men and head back into the pass to check on Cronin and Tavalori. If you find Igrayn and Ash along the way, tell them to meet me at the mouth of the pass," Erik ordered.

"And what of me?" Freeaxe asked.

"Will you make camp here or elsewhere?"

"We will take a position against the stone-face to the west," the Sire answered.

"Then we will set pickets around that," Erik replied.

He bowed and then moved back to his horse.

How easily people follow your lead if you take the right tone and issue commands like you know what you are talking about.

Taking to the saddle, he called his men around him and moved north, the battlefield a ruin behind him.

CHAPTER EIGHT

RELAN AND SAFFRON

Watch and be wary at this thing I am about to do. If you have a protest then break your silence now for the doom of nature is at hand.

Waves exploded against the dark shoals of the peninsula, the winter snow whipping around Relan as he stood against the wind. He clutched his staff tightly in his hand, his eyes staring out into the grey waves.

Sixteen hours, but they have come at last.

The black hulls rose and fell in the throes of the murky storm, nearly fifty vessels strong among the whitecaps that hammered against their passing.

He had watched them come on, their course unchecked as they fought against the elements, their bellies deep in the waves.

This is a fleet bound for war and conquest, and they are heavy with the steel of their arms.

Sucking a deep breath of icy air into his lungs, he shook off the ache in his muscles and studied the lead ship as it moved close to the shoals. Against the gale, he called out into the grey of the sea and sky.

"Ice and sea,
Sea and air,
Clash now without relent,
To prove your dominance over one another."

Around him the world exploded as the sea rose and the wind pitched. Driving ice and snow rained from the low clouds, the water sucking and whirling like a drowning man seeking to take what breath he could down with him when he sank.

Out in the straits, men scrambled with rigging and tattered sails, the fleet now tossed like a child's toy in a brass bathtub. The howling storm carried the screams of crewmen as they struggled against the very elements that granted them prosperity.

In the end your mighty struggles are all in vain…

The distant thunder of the first cracking timbers greeted him within ten minutes of his arcane call. The fleet slowly began to break apart from the power of his unnatural, channeled fury. Raising his staff still higher, he brought down lighting to illuminate the waves and fire the top of the ships' masts like candles in the dusky afterglow of each impact.

Snow and ice gained footing on the railings and decks of the heavily loaded vessels. The more the waves rocked and spun, the more ships tipped and capsized in the turbulent sea. From somewhere above, a vortex formed in the clouds as the wind swirled around itself and drew cold air from the heavens down onto the already frigid sea. Exhausted lungs froze as temperatures dropped so low the churning waves were tipped with ice as they slashed the wooden ships like sabers.

Sailors froze at their posts, becoming white statues bowed before the violence of the hurricane, and still Relan did not relent. He called the depths to twist and drag the ships down into their cavernous bellies. Churning whirlpools each the size of ten caravels opened and devoured anything still clinging to life on the surface.

It was a storm like nothing the straits had ever witnessed, and within the span of an hour only Relan was left alone upon the rocks, no living thing left on the surface of the sea. Around him the waves splashed and tore against the rocks, and the wind blew snow along the wooded shore, but no ship still sailed the waters of the grey sea.

Lowering his staff, he leaned heavily on it as he made his way back to the trees, his path erratic and his feet leaden. Within the woods he collapsed and whispered for the protections of his Oak Father as he lay down to sleep and recover his strength. His staff glowed, the firebirds warming his frozen body as he drew into his cloak and closed his eyes.

For now the Wintertide was safe, and if I've been devout I might find a permanent home among these shaded groves and green topped hills. But the goddess across the water will know what I've done and this will not be the last of her power to cross this ocean. A new threat is certain to be aimed at me.

Saffron awoke, the fire a heap of grey ash and her clothing crisp and hard with dried blood. She stood, fingers feeling along her abdomen but no scar was to be found. The skin was smooth and warm.

Another miracle, as my blade has done perfect work on my flesh. I seem to be getting my share of those lately, so the fates must be with me.

Wilam's tattered and torn corpse still lay in the center of the floor but not a drop of blood could be seen around it. She walked to the body, her boots echoing on the flags.

Sheathing her blade, she reached down and picked up her half-brother, only skin and bones left to carry weight.

Whatever touched you, it made you worse than your nature truly was. I remember some kindness in you, and I'll not let you lay here like a murdered rogue in your own house.

She carried his remains through the keep, out to the western balconies and, with a heave, threw them into the crashing waves of the bay below.

Rest in peace my kin, and may whoever did this to our house fall prey to a curse upon theirs as well.

Turning, she made for the Queen's gallery, wind tearing at her as she went and snow collecting on the roves of the city below. A peahen skittered from a shrub and Saffron jumped, hand on hilt before it slipped away and she continued on.

The apartments of the ladies-in-waiting were closed, but she removed a hidden key from behind a false stone and entered through a servant's door. It was cold inside, the fires unlit and the furniture covered with sheets, although some still lay exposed.

They left in a hurry, but at least that means they weren't murdered here.

She made her way to her rooms, the dresser and wardrobe both full. She quickly disrobed, found her sturdiest set of clothes, and redressed. Her reflection caught her eyes as she passed the mirror and she stopped to stare.

I'm death come to life.

The girl whose reflection she'd looked upon a handful of days before was no more. Where she'd always been lean now her bones were exposed, and her green eyes were rimmed with dark circles. Her hair, always unadorned, was now a tangle of knots and wild strands. Dirt and blood stained her cheeks in a kind of macabre mask, and she finally looked away.

The end of the line indeed.

Reattaching her sword, she threw on a fur-lined cloak and slipped from the room, her stomach churning with hunger.

She moved first to the rooms of the other ladies, each one half bare and signs of a hasty exit obvious in unfolded clothes and open drawers. In Verin's room she found a note cast on the bed and she picked it up as she stopped her search.

A list was scrawled out on it, things to be taken, and in one corner the word Alaon was scribbled in a hasty hand.

Alaon. The Queen's retreat in the south.

Tucking the note in her belt, she made her way from the rooms into the servants stair and then down into the kitchens. These too were nearly bare, but she found some milk still cold in the seaside cool boxes, as well as some stale bread and a handful of beans in a jar upon a window sill.

She ate all she could, draining the milk near the bottom, and then packed what remained of the bread in a pocket sewn into the inside of her cloak.

I'm alone, but I have a bearing and that is all I can ask. If the Queen still lives, I'll find her and then seek Igrayn if it is within my power.

Moving from the room, she exited the Queen's keep and moved back down the slopes toward the city, the snow coming down hard around her and a storm raging in the straights far out to the south sea.

CHAPTER NINE

ERIK

When I was a child my brother went with my father on campaign against the forces of the Jackal God in a place called the Thunder Fields. I remember him leaving, the way he looked upon his warhorse, both of them clad in shining mail, the standard of our house held in his right hand.

He never looked at me as he rode out with the honor guard, neither did my father, but my sister Amanda held my hand when I tried to follow after them, her grip keeping me in line until they were gone.

I often asked myself why I wanted to go. What did war hold that I thought was so desirable when I was seven? I know now that the immortality of youth clouds your judgment.

When my brother returned, he was changed. He no longer smiled, he didn't play with me, and when he finally took a wife some years later he chose to receive her alone rather than have me stand as his second.

I suppose I can't blame him for that. My exploits were already well known about the city. But it stung nonetheless. Still, after everything I've seen since the night of his wedding, I know why he kept me at arm's length. Battle is best kept from those you love, but the hand of fate saw to it that his sacrifice was in vain, as I now sit in the middle of a war of my own choosing.

Erik watched wisps of snow dance on the breeze like white fairies playing amid the deep groves of his father's forests. Behind him, Igrayn rode with Ash napping behind her, the Eldaryn's soft breathing having an almost hypnotic effect on those around him.

Tall Hills was a strange land, a place where barren rock gave way to tilled winter wheat fields. Small stone-and-thatch cottages clung along ridgelines or streambeds that snaked from the hills, giving some cold irrigation to the rocky land of the southern Aflyrian inlands. All the farms they passed were abandoned, some ransacked by Delvers, but others intact with only slight signs of a hurried departure by the families who once called them home.

"How is Malcolm?" he asked.

Ash stirred, said something unintelligible, and then went back to sleep. Igrayn sighed and said, "He will heal, with my prayers and those of Ash, I believe he will make a recovery within a fortnight."

Behind them Tavalori coughed. The woodsman rode close, a collection of Delver scalps hanging from his saddle, and his bow across his saddlehorn.

"Are you well?" Erik asked.

Tavalori nodded, his cloak pulled up around his face. Erik noticed that the man's strange taint was now present even when the breeze tried to clear it.

The Ghost Moon appeared from the steely clouds over the eastern hills, its pale face looking out of place in the late afternoon. The sun had yet to set in the violet west, but the winter brought the two celestial bodies into close contact, with only the late rising Blood Moon still hiding from the light of day.

"The night comes, but we've many more hours to the fortress," he said.

"Will you camp?" Igrayn asked.

"Yes, we'll travel till dusk, take a few hours, and then find a way to Nehru before the sun calls on a new day. We cannot risk Delver scouts reporting our presence while we camp all night this close to their ranges."

Ash stirred, and his voice was a groan, "Have we not arrived? I fear my hind quarters will never recover from all these days on horse."

"Keep your chin up, Friar. We'll be at the fortress before morning," Erik said.

"Assuming the fortress is even there," he commented as he sorely adjusted his seating.

Igrayn shook her head and Erik sighed, saying, "There will be battle, but the force left for the siege is not the host we fought in Tall Hills."

"And we lost a third of our number in the assault, so that doesn't bring me cheer," Ash observed.

"You did not have to come," Igrayn countered.

Ash looked first at Tavalori and then at Erik, saying, "No, but I felt it was my duty to accompany a lady in such hostile territory."

"Then your duty should also be to ride without complaint," Igrayn replied.

Ash gave a sigh, "Indeed."

"We could use your luck, however, so I'm grateful to have you," Erik said.

"If luck I can bring, I will continue with my prayers as we ride," Ash said.

Igrayn shook her head, and Erik looked back toward the south, the road twisting away into the growing gloom of evening.

Luck would be a welcome addition, or perhaps a little pyromancy if placed correctly, but as of now I'll have to rely on the strength in my arm and the desire in my heart for a quick victory.

No cook fires burned in the camp, and the pickets were set by the time Erik had finished grooming SmokeShadow and made his way back to the tent gifted him by Sire FreeAxe.

As he entered, the cold wind of the inland hills was replaced by the warmth of a brazier and the smell of the Kin cave tobacco smoking from Braxus's clay pipe. The mercenary's mud-covered boots were to the right of the entrance next to his patched and discolored traveling cloak.

"In the morning we prove our mettle again," Braxus said, after taking a long draw on his new pipe.

"I wouldn't waste that entire weed bag tonight. The Kin likely won't part with it as easily tomorrow, and we're a long way from the tobacco fields of Dravaria," Erik said as he removed his boots.

Braxus gave a grunt. "I might not be around tomorrow to enjoy it, so I tend to use up what I gain as quickly as I can."

Erik nodded.

True enough, the life of a mercenary is one that will end at any given hour.

"Have you checked on Malcolm since we made camp?" Erik asked.

"Yes. The field surgeons say the prayers of our resident believers have eased his wounds but he'll have to stay among the reserves come tomorrow and even then only for protection. He'll not be holding a weapon," Braxus answered.

"Good news I guess," he replied.

Erik slumped down into his sleeping furs and grabbed at a skin of wine hanging from one of the tent's supports next to him. Taking a long drink, he scratched the patch of hair at his chin and waved to Braxus for the pipe. Braxus handed the weed over with a grin.

After a long puff from the pipe, Erik lay back and gave a sigh.

"When this is done, I want you to go with Cronin into the highlands and find as many swords as those hills can provide," Erik said.

"You think Cronin hasn't already done that? He brought near a thousand to the battle already," Braxus said.

"He only had a couple of days, travelling on foot, to get that many, and even then only in the south of those sprawling hills. Now that he's done so, however, word has surely spread, and whichever clans remain will already be preparing for war in case the Delvers defeat us and come north in force."

Braxus nodded, "I guess that makes sense."

"Whatever happens tomorrow, a huge force of Ruks and Delvers has already slipped through the Yule into the East and will be marching toward ChanderNagor. Their first stop will be Iropa, then every other coastal town they can raze and loot until they make the capital. This attack could delay them, and perhaps give us enough time." Erik continued.

"Time for what?" Braxus asked.

"To raise an army of our own and get to ChanderNagor before them."

Braxus sat up, "You mean to join NyWinter?"

Erik lay back and took another long puff on his pipe, saying, "Only time will tell…"

The Western Fortress of Nehru was a black silhouette cast against the crimson stain of the waning Blood Moon. Its golden tower lights flickered like enchanted eyes looking down into the black valley below.

The Kin were already down the slope, and Erik's remaining cavalry, now just barely over two hundred strong, waited with Cronin's infantry along high road.

"I'm feeling lucky," Braxus said.

There was a tingle in Erik's skin and whatever cloud that had plagued his thoughts the night before lifted. Braxus had a strange definition of "luck," but this time Erik believed him. He turned, and Ash smiled at him from behind Igrayn's saddle.

"I think we've been blessed," Erik said.

"Well that's a neat trick," Braxus replied.

Below, the clash of arms sounded and a horn blew. Erik drew *Fury* and set SmokeShadow to a gallop. The cavalry closed ranks behind him, Igrayn falling back and Telluria taking her place at the head of the charge.

"What art will you provide today?" Erik called over the sound of the advance.

"Globes," Telluria answered.

Erik turned, but the Wizard was looking straight ahead, her cheeks touched with blue and her green eyes aglow.

Pressing his heels into SmokeShadow's flank, he urged more speed, two more horns blowing in the conflagration before them and a bell sounding from the keep's tower. To the east, the pale grey sky burst to life, the dawn illuminating the field as Telluria waved her hand and seven silver globes rose from the ground inside the Delver defense.

Ruks shouted and cracked whips, but the Delvers fell away from the globes as each grew to the size of a farmer's market cart.

The Kin pressed against the enemy line, those Delvers who saw the globes breaking ranks and the Kin took advantage all along the front.

Telluria snapped her first closed and then opened it with a dramatic flair, the globes on the field below exploding in a million blades of ice. Delvers and Ruks fell by the score, the entire enemy center shattered, and the Kin pouring over those who remained in a dark tide.

"Riders!" Erik called.

Braxus blew a horn and the cavalry charged into the mix, the Delver encampment already a tangle of broken platoons and chaos. Ruks and Delvers fell in droves before the charge and the Kin felled what remained.

Closer to the keep, Ruks rallied several hundred Delvers along the siege line, and Erik pulled his cavalry back as Cronin and his hillmen ran through the dead with furious screams and weapons raised.

Erik watched them hammer into the new Delver ranks, their numbers overwhelming. The monstrous Freeaxe, shape-changed to resemble lizard-kin, found him, his female vanguard with him, each of them decorated with the blood of battle.

"Another pocket lies to the east along the broken walls of the East Keep and I've sent my sons down there," Sire Freeaxe said.

"Will they be enough?" Erik asked.

"It's their will to show their power. Those who remain may become full Sires after this campaign, so they will do as they do," the Sire replied.

"I'll send lancers nonetheless, to see that no Delver escapes, and hunters to check the eastern pass," Erik said.

Freeaxe nodded and moved off, Braxus coming close as Telluria watched the battle unfolding at the siege works.

"I'll lead the lancers. It's the best way to see it gets done right," Braxus said.

"Good! Take thirty men, but leave Rikov. I'll need him since Malcolm isn't available," Erik said.

Braxus saluted and rode off, Telluria urging her horse forward.

"Another victory for Sir Tall Hills," she observed.

"You make it easy to be victorious," he replied.

"Magic is a dangerous business, but not every battle will be like this. One day soon there will be arcane power on the other side of the field, and then you will see if I'm really worth your praise," she said.

"You're a strange one," he said.

"Why do you say that?"

"Just the way you think, and because when we first entered Mahe I thought you wanted me, and yet you seem to be directing me to Igrayn," he answered.

"Who says I still don't want you?"

He watched her, but she didn't turn to face him. The smell of the sea drifted in, and the green at the ends of her hair were now frosted with ice.

"Your element would drown me," he said.

She shook her head, "No, that's a folk tale. In the end we are all the same in the flesh, although creating offspring is probably out of the question."

"Offspring… are you serious?"

"I'm just stating a fact, but I'll not pursue a course that isn't open to me, and as Igrayn is my friend, I'll not stand in the way of her destiny because of some simple desire of my own."

Erik shivered.

Wizards! A power that is beyond anything I wish to truly know, no matter how lovely the packaging around it.

The Great Gate of Nehru had finally granted them entrance after more than an hour's wait, and Erik's men were warm with anger by the time they spurred their exhausted mounts beyond the stone maw of the western keep.

A sallow-eyed group of men-at-arms greeted them, a man in half plate at their head.

"To whom do we owe the debt of our salvation?" the armored man asked.

"The Legion of Mahe, the Kin of Araba'Duur, and the men of the Yule inlands," Erik answered.

"Mahe? Then you are under the command of Sir Ector?" the man asked.

"No, the defense of Mahe was abandoned, but that is a long story and we are weary from travel and war," Erik said.

The man nodded, "Yes, I'm sorry, please bring your men inside the hall. We've little to offer other than shelter and a fire, but that is yours for the taking."

Erik dismounted, Telluria, Igrayn, and Ash following suit with the remainder of his lancers.

"I see people within the inner courtyard. It looks like some kind of camp," Ash whispered.

"It must be the farmers and their families from the homesteads we saw along the way," Igrayn replied.

Erik nodded as he moved SmokeShadow along a path cut between the sleeping tents and makeshift homes inside the massive inner court. People watched the riders pass, tending their small fires, their eyes dark under heavy cloaks and blankets. Somewhere a baby cried and a dog barked from the fortress kennels.

"Rikov, find the men beds, tend to the horses, and be sure the friar is brought to a place of prayer," Erik commanded.

"But," Ash began.

Erik turned to him and whispered, "I need to know what's happening in the fortress, and only a disciple of Bandylegs could do the job I need."

Ash looked at Igrayn, then back at him before he nodded.

"The chapel is this way. I can have Korg show you," the plated man offered.

Ash went with one of the men-at-arms, Erik turning to his host, saying, "There is much to discuss, and I would see that done quickly but my bones are weary."

"Indeed, I will give you my own chambers and have food prepared from our remaining reserves. With the siege ended, we can begin resupplying our larders tomorrow," the man said.

"Thank you, Sir…"

"Rolak Thane," the man offered.

"Sir Thane, I will take you up on your offer. Can you see the ladies are provided rooms as well?"

Thane bowed, "It shall be done."

Nodding, Erik followed the man into the main bastion, Kin horns blowing the all clear from beyond the walls.

The water was warm as he splashed it on his face from a bowl, a fire burning in the hearth and the room quiet. His scale armor lay on the bed, as did his grime-stained undershirt. The smell of battle and hard weeks in the saddle clung to him, and he brought water to his face again with a sigh.

What I wouldn't give for a hot bath.

He scrubbed his stubble-covered cheeks, took a cloth and wiped his chest, neck, and then under his arms before casting it aside.

I've finally got a comfortable place to lay my head but I don't feel like sleep.

Standing, he paced around the room, found a wool robe and threw it over his shoulders.

I think it's time to confront Igrayn about a few things...

He walked to the door, opened it, and checked the hall. It was empty, torches guttering along the walls and he slipped out with bare feet.

I wonder if Shera would hear me? Of course she would, no matter how quiet I was, she always heard me slipping out of my room.

Two doors down, he stopped, his hand going to the handle before a sound came from within. Leaning to the wood, he listened and heard something break and the grunt of a man.

He tried the handle but a bolt had been thrown on the far side.

"Igrayn!" he yelled.

There was another curse, and movement on the far side. He threw his shoulder into the door but it held fast, the wood heavy and reinforced with cross bars and studs.

"Guards!" he called down the hall.

From somewhere below boots and clanking mail echoed up. He banged on the door, his fire welling up inside him as there was a heavy thud of overturned furniture beyond the frame.

"Igrayn!" he yelled again.

Up the hall two men in chain appeared, short blades in hand.

"We need this door open now!"

They stared at him a moment, and he yelled again, "Get something to break it down!"

The two scrambled away and he turned back to the door but silence reined on the far side.

He pressed his head against the wood, fire burning in his chest. A minute passed and then the bolt was thrown and the door slid open.

Igrayn stood on the far side, lip bleeding, eye swollen, and a hand pressed against her side where blood dripped from her tattered nightdress. She looked at him, tried to say something, and then fell forward.

He caught her, hands trembling as he picked her up and carried her from the door. The guards returned before he made it to his room, a length of heavy wood in their hands set with iron rungs.

"See to the room, I'll take care of her," he said.

They ran past, and he slipped inside his room, moved to that bed and laid her gently on it. Reaching out, he grabbed *Fury* from its sheath and placed it in her hand as he held on as well.

"Fury..." he whispered.

Time slowed around them, a golden glow stretching out from the blade as a wave of healing washed over them.

Igrayn's eyes fluttered open, her lip mending and the swelling in her eye returning to normal. She took a deep breath, rising from the bed like a viper, but he caught her, his arms holding her for a moment before she stopped struggling.

"How?" she whispered.

"I have magic, although I keep it to myself when I can," he replied.

She turned to him, eyes emerald and the smell of the sea mingling with the heat of his internal fire.

"It was Raziel," she said.

"Raziel? Here?" he asked.

"Yes, he came dressed as one of Cronin's hillmen, a beard on his cheeks and scarves about his head. I didn't recognize him at first, but when he spoke I knew in an instant," she said.

Raziel, once bodyguard, then murderer of priests in the Temples of Mahe, and now an assassin...

"What happened?" Erik asked.

She shook her head, "He could have killed me, should have, but he wanted something more before he sent me to my goddess."

Fire burned inside Erik, and Igrayn drew close, her water warmed by the power of his spark.

"I killed him." she finished.

That's the way with close combat, odds are both parties will die. But Raziel didn't have my magic to save him.

"Why would he come for you, why risk it?" Erik asked.

She shook her head but never left his chest, "I don't know. He was my protector, the man my father assigned to see me through my journey."

"A journey only a fool would allow in the first place," Erik added.

She pulled away, the magic to the blade slowly subsiding and her eyes held a hard edge that wasn't there before.

"My father is a great man!"

"Your father allowed the prize of his kingdom's treaty with Aflyr to leave his lands with an assassin. I dare say that doesn't qualify as all that great in my book," Erik replied. He knew that it was his fear speaking, but somehow it only came out as anger.

She tried to slap him but he caught her wrist and she cursed and pulled away.

"Who are you to speak to me like that?" she hissed.

The smell of the sea was strong, and her face was ghostly pale.

"I'm certainly not Raziel, who would accept abuse from a spoiled little girl!"

"Bastard!" she screamed.

Two guards entered, followed by Telluria, the Wizard holding her staff at the ready.

"What's going on?" Telluria asked.

"I was just saving the princesses life," Erik said.

"Liar, I saved my own life, as Raziel's body will attest. Take no credit where it isn't due," Igrayn spat.

I want to hate her but for some reason I want her all the more when she's furious.

"Raziel?" Telluria asked.

"It's a long story, but as I obviously had no part in it, I'll let Her Highness tell you the tale," Erik said.

He pushed past the guards and Telluria, *Fury* still in his grasp. Grabbing his belt and scabbard from a post at the door, he walked down into the hall. He was three doors away when he heard the first sobs, and he sighed, his hands fastening his belt as he took the steps toward the great hall two by two.

Near the bottom Braxus met him, the mercenary still covered in the grime of war.

"Going somewhere?" Braxus asked.

Erik pulled up, saying, "Remember what I said about going with Cronin?"

"Yeah."

"I want you to go tomorrow, leave Rikov here to man the garrison, and tell Sire Freeaxe I'll meet him in Ixprys in eight days, along with you and Cronin."

"What? Erik, you're not making any sense. What happened?" Braxus asked.

"I'm going to Mahe," Erik replied.

"Mahe? You'll never make it to Ixprys if you go to Mahe. I mean I'll be pressed to get to Ixprys that fast and my route is direct up the Yule spine," Braxus said.

"Let me worry about that. Just give my regards to Sir Thane, have Rikov keep an eye on him, and have Malcolm go with the Kin," Erik continued.

"I still don't understand..." Braxus began.

Erik cut him short, saying, "Just do it! You've got to trust me."

Braxus nodded and Erik patted him on the shoulder, then fled down the final few steps. When he entered the hall he marched across it until he slipped into an alcove and pressed his back against the cold stone.

If I'm going to do this, it has to be now, no matter what she feels about me.

He reached inside a long leather tube in the back of his belt and pulled out a wand of dark wood, etched with nine winged horses.

You have travelled with me a long time, my prize of Asjgard, and I've nursed your gifts as best I could, but now I must use another of the pegasi from this enchanted stable.

Holding the wand aloft, he pictured the Palace of Mahe in his mind's eye and whispered one word.

"There..."

In a flash the alcove was gone and in its place was a gilded room overlooking a stormy sea. Erik returned the wand – now marked with only eight winged horses carved in the wood – back to its secret holder and fell into the covers of a large bed, his eyes closing as exhaustion finally dragged him into a fitful slumber.

CHAPTER TEN

ERIK

Yes, I ran. Men run don't they? Well, some men do, and I know I can dress it up any way I like, say that it was "for a cause," but at my core I know the truth. I ran because I couldn't protect her, I ran because of the hurt in her eyes, and I ran because when it comes right down to it I've always taken the easy route and fled responsibility.

My problem now is that I didn't run far enough. I could have used the magic to return to haunted and cursed Taux, to Shera, but instead in a panic I came back to Mahe. I guess I could flee Igrayn, but something in my spirit wouldn't let me flee Alfyr.

Maxus was true to his word, and once I was discovered in the palace, and the victory at Nehru had been reported, he set the investiture in play. By tomorrow I'll be Duke Erik of Mahe, sovereign of the West. The city is abuzz with the news, and a full revolt already in play against any remaining bureaucracy left in place by King NyWinter.

The people were starved for a hero, a king, and I've fallen perfectly into their lofty dreams, but I fled once again to the only place I knew I could go. But I have not fled to freedom, for my new title is just another kind of trap.

The water steamed as it poured through his hair and then down his forehead. Erik could smell the lavender-scented soap as it mixed with the cinnamon-laced candles burning around the bath chamber.

"I'll have to buy a new bathing tub, as this one will never again be clean." Bianca said.

The Lady DeWinter, daughter of the Master of Trades and a one-night conquest after his victory in Mahe Palace, placed the porcelain pitcher on the slate floor and, with delicate care, brought a wet cloth to Erik's face. She wiped the excess water from his brow, and tilting his head first left, then right, she let the water drain.

Erik smiled, his eyes closed and his body relaxed in the hot water.

"War is a dirty business," he observed.

"And a dangerous one it would seem," she said, her hand sliding down his arm as she drew an imaginary line from bruise to bruise to bruise.

Erik opened his eyes and tried to focus on the upside-down image of the merchant's daughter who sat behind him on a stool. She was looking at his body with narrow eyes, her lips drawn tight.

If only that was true concern on her face, but I know her spies had already informed her of my ascendance even before I arrived on her doorstep. That alone is what allowed me entrance a second time. Still, she is one of the last souls of noble blood left in Mahe, even is diluted by generations away from ChanderNagor, so I'll accept her illusions of comfort and affection if it is offered.

"I'm in better condition than I look to be," he said.

She shook her head and found his eyes, a smirk turning up the corner of her mouth.

"Truly?" she asked.

"You are welcome to experiment," he answered.

She laughed at that, her washcloth again going about the business of cleaning the grime that had found its way into every fiber of his flesh.

"I've told you before that I would not again entertain you until you gained a higher position," she said.

Closing his eyes again, he said. "There are many positions I might imagine that could fill that statement."

She splashed him, and he covered his face with both hands, the defense spilling water onto the stone floor.

"I am a lady, Sir!" Bianca defended in mock hurt.

"And a feisty one at that," Erik laughed.

Behind him, Bianca stood and straightened the half-strung bodice of her dressing gown before moving to a full-length, slivered mirror that was framed with two heavy velvet curtains.

"What should I wear this evening?" she asked, clearly changing the subject while also staying on her favorite topic: herself

She turned back and forth, her eyes taking stock of her appearance in the reflective surface.

"What you have on is wonderful from where I sit," Erik said.

Play at this bravado, fool! It does little to assuage the hurt in your soul for Igrayn.

Taking up a bar of soap, he began a second round of cleaning. Bianca waved his comment off, turning to the side and running a delicate hand down her stomach.

"I thought you might return, you know," she said absently.

Erik raised an eyebrow. "You did, huh?"

"Yes, and a lady always prepares for such things if she is to capture every moment with the utmost of tact," she replied.

"Lady DeWinter, *you* prepare for everything. You've studied court life to the extent that you know thrice as much as a woman with twice your years," Erik said.

"And I will marry thrice as well for it," she added.

Erik stopped his cleaning at this, his eyes returning to the lovely, curvaceous woman before the mirror.

"And you think I might help you in such a thing?" he asked innocently.

She finally looked from her own image back to him, her face set with the same deadly calm his own visage held.

"I wouldn't marry you even if you were the King of Aflyr, as I fear you are forever beneath me," she smiled.

Erik smiled back, their humor playing like two snakes taking each other in.

"Beneath you, atop you...it matters not to me, but you overstate your social status if you believe you are higher born than a Duke."

He leaned back into the bath, adding, "Besides, I have my sights set on better fields to set my plow."

"Well, at least we understand each other. But no matter what we feel, I'm the only one in this city with highborn blood enough to legitimize your claim to a throne. Remember that," she said, her shadow swiftly following behind her as she slipped from the room.

Erik stared up at the heavy-beamed ceiling.

Well, you've done it again. Now if only I could get Telluria alone perhaps I'd find a way to destroy my relationship with her and be done with women all together...

The offices of the Regent were very similar to what Erik remembered from three weeks before, other than the presence of a mess of maps and parchment that had grown tenfold.

"Regent," Erik said as he entered the room, a legionnaire at his left shoulder.

Behind the oak desk, Commander Maxus sat with his legion jacket open and his undershirt unlaced.

"Sir Tall Hills," Maxus said without looking up, his attention still on some matter inside a freshly-pressed scroll.

Erik walked across the floor, his newly polished boots making a squeaking sound as he did so. Behind him, the legionnaire gave a salute and shut the door, leaving the two men alone. Staying at attention, Erik stood in the legion Captain's uniform that had been given to him upon his return from Lady DeWinter's abode.

Maxus continued to read another minute before finally shaking his head and leaning back in his chair. Running a hand through his salt and pepper hair, the man eyed Erik before with a blank expression.

"I do not have the time to play games, so I will get right to the point of the matter," Maxus began.

"By all means," Erik nodded.

"My men tell me that you are a Kin-friend, and that the Sire of Araba'duur has drafted an alliance with you," Maxus said.

Erik nodded again.

Maxus watched him closely, the fingers on his left hand strumming several times on the surface of the desk in nervous contemplation.

"What is your game here?" Maxus said at last.

Erik gave him another smile, this one very similar to the one he had exchanged with Bianca.

"I have no plan, save that I feel these people deserve better than the foolish leadership they currently have," Erik responded.

Maxus raised a bushy eyebrow.

"You don't say?" Maxus mumbled.

Erik continued to smile.

"Commander, you know as well as I that the King has abandoned Mahe. His desire for self-preservation has sacrificed the rest of his country, all to protect his throne and the jewel of his kingdom: ChanderNagor. I came to this land seeking only to improve my swordsmanship and fill my meager purse, but as things unfolded I realized I could not stand by and watch as Aflyr was laid waste by Delver blades.

"My company and I found we had a chance to save Mahe if we freed your men from their prison in time. Once that was done, I knew my next chance to help Aflyr lay in the south. With your help I was able to destroy an invading army at Tall Hills and free the Fortress of Nehru before it too fell into Ruk hands. Yet while I traipse all throughout his kingdom, *King* NyWinter sits in ChanderNagor on his gilded throne and waits for the enemy to come to *him*, all so that he might make some grand display of victory," Erik explained.

Maxus became visibly angry at the mention of the king's name.

"Then tell me, once this war is done what will you do?" Maxus asked.

Erik stood a moment, his smile never fading.

"I will represent the best interests of Aflyr to the King and hope that he listens to reason, that is, unless something unfortunate happens to him before then," Erik finished.

Maxus tried hard to conceal a smile.

"I see. Then as Lord Commander of the Cursed Legion, I will continue with the plans already set in place. On this evening I will raise you to the station of Lord Erik of Tall Hills, Duke of Mahe," Maxus stated.

Erik bowed his head, but his eyes still held questions. "I have a confession, Commander, my name is Fleetwood."

"Fleetwood? That's not an Aflyrian name. Unless names themselves have changed more than I thought from my time out of time," Maxus replied.

"It's not Aflyrian, it's Thalonian, and although I deceived you with my claim of being an Aflyrian Knight, I do hold the blood of noble knights and kings of the north," Erik admitted.

Maxus sighed, "I knew your tale was copious at best, but I had little choice other than to give you the chance to prove your worth. As you've done that, I would forgive such a transgression, as I assume the people of this city would as well. In my mind, a noble is a noble, be he from Aflyr or Thalania."

"Thalonia," Erik corrected.

"Does it really matter now?"

"No," Erik replied softly.

"You already have the people, as do all the members of the Company of the Coast. The citizens of Mahe believe you saved them from certain doom, and you very well may have. Where noble blood is concerned, I think I have that issue now solved as well," Maxus continued.

"Do tell," Erik prompted.

Maxus frowned.

"It seems the King forgot to gather up all those of royal blood in Mahe during his final call. It has come to my attention that a relative of his family is still in the city. Are you in any way familiar with the Lady Bianca DeWinter?" Maxus asked.

Erik tried hard not to flush, his demeanor hard while maintaining his smile.

"I believe I've met her," Erik replied.

Maxus nodded.

"Good, then this should not be difficult. I will have her oversee your elevation, and with someone of royal blood as witness, the motion should carry over to the scribes and bureaucrats who have already begun flooding me with requests and desires," Maxus finished, his large hands waving over his cluttered desk.

"Then I look forward to the ceremony tonight," Erik confirmed. With a crisp click of his booted heels, he bowed to the Commander and moved to exit the hall.

"Do not make me regret this Lord Fleetwood," Maxus said before Erik could exit the room.

Erik turned back one last time, his hand on the door.

"When we are done, Commander, Aflyr will be better for it," Erik promised.

Both men locked eyes for a moment and then nodded. Today had been a watershed, and both of them knew it.

THE
MID-WINTER FALL

BOOK II

CHAPTER ONE

RELAN

*I*t is whispered among the boughs of the trees in the north that once Belmarilian, my master and Heirophant of Cabal of the Order of Druids, destroyed an army of Delvers fifty-thousand strong for the Prince of the Lupin Hills. Years later, when the prince was the High Priest of the God's Spire, Belmarilian came to collect on that debt but was denied. Days later, a rain of elemental fire destroyed the city, but left the High Priest alive as an example of what happens when a soul goes against the will of the Druids.

In total, over one-hundred thousand lives have been lost to the power of my Order, ten times that which I have destroyed in the past week, and yet my hands cannot seem to be rid of the stain of blood I find there.

This is what it is like to play a game between two gods, for Belmarilian is most certainly one of their number, and the Arcanian goddess of suffering who sired his heir will not stop with a drowned fleet or a frozen army. Surely she is already on the move, probably in Aflyr among Humanity.

I could stay here, among the white trees of the Wintertide and delay a report to the Hierophant, but in the end he would know what I have done, or not done. He is called 'The Watcher' for a reason. So I must continue on, into lands where I am a foreign entity and my power is lessoned by both civilization and the dashing currents of so many elemental-born souls.

Frost, white and crystalline, lay around Relan in a perfect circle as he rose from the bed of brown leaves and dusky grass. Above, the blue sky was painted with streaks of wispy clouds, and the skeletal trees held a coating of glittering snow.

He could hear the surf, waves crashing against rocks beyond the trees as he pulled his fur cloaks closer around his shoulders and closed his eyes. The sound of snapping timbers and truncated screams still whispered in his ears, but he rose, steadying his legs with the Phoenix Staff.

The firebirds glowed, tiny eyes ablaze with shining rubies, and the warmth of the artifact saturated his muscles.

Turning toward the rising sun, he moved from his warm circle into the frigid morning. The grass and leaves crunched under his bare feet, water beading on his toes as he made his way through the trees.

At mid-day he took his rest beside a stream where thin membranes of ice circled smooth stones. As he ate, he watched sparrows play amid the snow in the limbs. Deer trails snaked through thick brown brush and he marked the prints of a Lowl hunting party that must have passed in the night.

When the sun trailed into the woods and shadows painted the trees grey, he took his rest beneath a sheltering pine. He drove his staff into the earth, listening to the sound of the pine needles crunching, and whispered words to the wind that drew the branches down into a shelter. Once enclosed, he brought forth his meager bounty, ate amid the smell of pine, and then drew his cloaks around him for sleep.

The morning broke quiet and shadowed, steely clouds hanging low over of the trees and a deep chill settling into the forest. There was little to eat other than pine shavings. These he chewed as he walked.

He disturbed a wolf pack an hour after the sun breached its zenith, the long-legged and white-coated creatures following him for the better part of the afternoon before they lost interest and slunk back into the undergrowth.

When he stopped for the night, a low cleft of rock and a burbling stream were his shelter and water-source. He lay still, staring up at tendrils of frost that collected on the rock above his head, forming from the white breath he released.

Saffron, the Knight of Lystbrook, drifted into his thoughts. Somewhere she was still out there, questing perhaps, but surely safe as he'd dispatched all the threats to her kingdom in the intervening days.

Even if he was free of her, there would be more civilization to deal with, be it from water-touched Corsairs or fire-blooded Humans. As he lay on the ground, the earth whispered words of slumber and he drifted off.

A tremor shook him awake, but when he opened his eyes he found the rock overhang gone and the smell of spring flowers drifting around him.

This is no dream… magic is at work.

He rose, reached for his staff and found only thick moss where he had left the weapon. From somewhere in the mist the sound of music drifted, pipes lilting and playing on through the air in a dulcet tune.

His feet sent waves of discomfort up his legs when he stood, the ground foreign and corrupting to his elements.

This is the second world, and if I am here then the trouble the region of Aflyr faces is greater than I could have imagined. Damnable fates, the goddess of suffering has gone beyond my line of foresight and cast a net against me even after I destroyed her army! Does she truly dare bring forth the ancient twins?

From beyond his line of vision, a laugh broke through the mist. He turned, but only a shadow could be seen as it drifted away into nothingness.

"You have accomplished what you desired. I am here, now tell me what this is about!" he called.

Another laugh was the only answer, and he clenched his jaw, eyes darting left and right as the sound of flowing water and wings flapping concealed the shadow stranger's location.

"Tell me your wish and be done with it, I have no time to play Fey games," he said.

Surely this is the work of the Fey, because a Dragon would not play so.

"What purpose do you serve, Great Druid?" a female voice asked.

He turned, but no one was behind him.

"I come in the service of my master in search of seeds lain in wait for the spring," he replied.

The laughter again, then, "Your seeds have already sprung, and your master knows this. Now the slumbers of the second world have been lifted by the very powers who put us down, and I am charged to find this seed."

"And what will you do when you find it?" he asked.

"Deliver it to the one of power who freed me. Then I can do as I please."

"If you believe that, then you are a fool."

"What choice have I? It is a risk, certainly, but a risk with a chance is one I will take rather than suffer and slumber."

Relan shook his head, whispered words of elemental wards that drifted into the oblivion of the fog.

My magic doesn't work here. The connection to the Oak Father is lost in the void.

"First, I must set you to the mists. Then I will find the would-be king and see him fall into the darkness of eternal rest as well."

"What have kings to do with any of this?" Relan asked.

"I must take his strength, remove him from the field, and when the Human kingdoms are in the hands of the one of power, the goddess, then I can seek out my better half," she laughed.

The Dragon.

"That is a terrible wish. The wyrm will not bow to you, just as it didn't in the old days," he said.

"Perhaps not, but chains can still bind it, and with all I have done to that point, it will not be able to stop me."

Relan leaned back, but his feet were held firm. He looked down, and realized that the moss had grown over his feet, wrapped his ankles and crawled up his legs.

"Your meddling is done, Druid, and I must use your power to slip the veil," she said.

The speaker appeared then, tall and shaded green with the shape of feline features and eyes as black as polished onyx. He struggled, but she moved close, long-fingered hands reaching out to grasp his cheeks as she drew his lips to hers. The power of the moss held him, her lips draining his essence and his mouth filling with the taste of dark corrupted earth. He choked, but she continued to probe his mouth with her long tongue, the combined sparks in his chest flaring and faltering with each second he was in her embrace.

Finally she pulled away and he staggered. He would have fallen but the moss rooted him in place like an emerald sheath.

She stood before him, now changed and radiant. Her skin like polished ivory, ears pointed and elegant, and her eyes blue as the spring sea in the archipelago. A film of sheer silk dressed her features, and the Phoenix Staff was held proudly in one graceful hand.

A smile touched her flawless face, and somewhere inside his tortured soul the spark of attraction was kindled.

"This won't do," she said.

Lifting the staff, she waved her hand over it and the tall artifact reshaped to that of a rod tipped at each end with a radiant azure gem.

"Yes, that is more like it. Now, keep yourself safe, Druid, for I will need your power again before this is done," she said.

He shook his head, a whisper hissing from his cracked lips. She frowned, tilting her head and leaning close.

"What?" she asked.

"The world is changed, fell one, and your power is not what you think it is," he said.

She drew back, the smile returning.

"Swords will not cut me, the talons of the wyrm will be like the aggression of a kit. No, Druid, my power is absolute in this backward and feral world, of that you can be certain," she finished.

Turning, she drifted into the mist, and Relan let his head fall, the moss keeping him like a wayward statue.

When you ruled the world it was a feral place, but now a power exists beyond your reckoning. I can only hope one of the water-born takes enough interest to appear, for their power might be able to stem the tide where mine could not.

CHAPTER TWO

IGRAYN

I have not wept since I was a child, but tonight I ached in such a way that there were never enough tears. I shed my tears for betrayal by my family, my defender, and the man I love...

No, I can't think that way. Not now, not when I am alone in this foreign country, abandoned by anyone and everyone I hold dear.

I could go to Tavalori, assuming Ash would allow it – which is doubtful. But to what purpose? Whatever desire I felt for him bled away with each passing day of this life-and-death struggle. It's funny how childish desires can evaporate in the face of death.

Now, my focus has shifted to the man I can't understand, the rogue, the noble, the knight, the enigma that is Erik.

What would you do spirit? I know you are there, as I've felt you like the specter of death since the assassination attempt last night by Raziel. Are you a shade of doom or some other power that has now turned its attention on me as this strange game of conflict plays out around me?

Telluria rose from the bed. At the sound, Igrayn's eyes opened with a flutter.

"What is it?" Igrayn asked.

Telluria was pale, the skin under her eyes touched with a shade of blue. The smell of the ocean was oppressive in the chamber.

"We must go." she replied.

Igrayn sat up, "What?"

Her friend was already standing, long-fingered hands gathering her robe from a hook on the wall, and her feet kicking off their slippers.

"Something is happening. The waters have been disturbed."

Igrayn shook her head, "I don't know what you're saying."

"If we don't go, if we don't make the offer, the balance will swing and the nation will be tipped into darkness."

Rising, Igrayn went to Telluria and took her by the arm. The Wizard turned, eyes blank and dull in their green depths.

She's asleep?

"Telluria," Igrayn said.

"He is awake, but without a sacrifice he'll not move against his darker half," she replied.

"Telluria!" Igrayn repeated, this time her voice rising.

The Wizard blinked, eyes clearing and a shuddering breath leaving her in a rush. There was a moment of confusion, and then she turned to Igrayn and fixed her with a look of power that made the hairs on the back of her neck stand on end.

"What did you hear?" Telluria asked.

"Something about a sacrifice," she answered.

Nodding, Telluria continued to collect her things, adding, "I've had a vision. Power is in play in Aflyr, and two ancients have been awakened. The darkness has gone to Mahe, but the light is here, among the snowy stone of these passes, and we must find him."

"I don't understand," Igrayn said.

Turning back to her, Telluria fixed that powerful gaze once more and let out a sigh, "Are you a princess of the people? Will you give up everything for them?"

Igrayn didn't reply, instead shaking her head as she took a step back. Telluria was quick as a viper, her hand snapping out to grab Igrayn before she could take another step..

"Tell me, or all is lost!"

"I…" Igrayn stammered.

"This is not a time for children, and surely we will all be tested in the fire, but I must know if you can take on the burden that is to come?"

Igrayn watched her a long moment, whatever fear she had draining away as she slowly shook her head.

"I will face the fire, as I am nothing but the will of my people," she replied.

Telluria nodded, "Good, then collect your things. The mountains call."

Shuddering, Igrayn did as she was told, the cold in the room settling into her bones even as she bundled against it.

"This is pure insanity!" Ash raged above the call of the wind.

Igrayn closed her eyes, the snow swirling around the rocks and the sky a steely shade of grey that stretched into darkness on the horizon.

Please give me the strength to endure this journey with him.

Heat bloomed along her back, and Ash shifted position, whispering words to his damnable deity. Beside them, astride a shaggy pony, sat Telluria, her pale face and frosted hair looking shining against the backdrop of the storm.

"It's not much farther. I can feel the pull of the universe like the sucking tide at your feet along the shore," the Wizard called.

Igryan nodded and leaned into her pony's neck, its smell coming into her nose and turning her stomach.

It feels like a week in this saddle, and yet only a day has passed since we left the confines of Nehru.

The snow continued to drift down, the mountains rising up like grey and white giants until Telluria's pony finally came to a halt and refused to go further.

"At least the mounts understand our danger," Ash whispered.

Telluria slid from the saddle and turned to a long snaking path of white that led in turn into a mist of cloud that had been sliced from the sky by the peaks and pooled into a billowing lake far above.

"The air grows thin, and we must hurry before our strength fails," Telluria urged.

Ash, pale as a ghost amid his coppery hair, wavered as Igrayn dropped to the snow but did not move.

"I'll stay with the ponies, as I fear my legs will not move in the frozen water sea around me," he said.

Igrayn nodded, reached up and pulled his cloak further over his small head, and then marched through a foot of powder to stand next to Telluria.

"We are going to die up here," Igrayn said.

Telluria nodded, "It is a distinct possibility, but the sacrifice is worth it, even if we never return."

"Perhaps, but I'll go no further without an explanation," Igrayn added.

Wind played against both women, their dark hair dancing as Telluria gave a sigh. "Do you know the legend of the twins?" she asked.

"Yes, my mother told me that tale when I was a child, as I assume most in the world do," Igrayn replied.

"Then can you imagine what it means when legends come to life, when the flow of time is disturbed and these powers come into play in the world of today?"

Igrayn shook her head, "Legends of the Fey and the Dragons are just that, play stories from the Age of Mists."

"No, that is what many believe, but these creatures are still here, most staying in a slumber for many lifetimes. On occasion something rouses them, and when that happens, ruin follows in their footsteps," Telluria replied.

Igrayn looked up into the mists, whispering, "Then have we come to kill a Fey?"

Telluria raised her staff, the blades glowing with an eerie light. "No, we have come to charm a Dragon."

Amid the haze of mists, the air was warm and a layer of condensation beaded on Igrayn's cheeks as she followed the glow of Telluria's staff. Around her feet, water rushed among the green, lichen-encrusted rocks as it made its way out into the true world beyond the white shroud.

Time bent in the fog, and a sense of fatigue pulled her down and weighed on her eyes. Only the draw of the staff's light kept her moving forward, Telluria occasionally speaking words that were lost in spiderwebs of confusion before they reached her mind.

The light pulsed, and she wandered with it, the sway taking on the aspect of the fireflies that lurked in the gardens of her mother's seaside estates. Darkness surrounded the golden glow, and she reached for it, but it leapt away.

For a moment her feet stood amid the water, but then she splashed forward, hand still outstretched as she made chase. Amid her movements, motes of deep blue hues sprang up, and then slipped away into oblivion. Still she kept forward, chasing the light.

Within the dark, the glow paused and she leapt at it, fingers grasping before it winked out of existence and she was tumbling through black oblivion. The impact at the bottom shook her bones, and stars spun in her eyes where the glow had once transfixed them.

Her breath came in great gasps, and she managed to get her arms underneath her enough to push her face from the ground. Moss squished beneath her fingers, the stone beneath solid and warm as she blinked away her daze until her vision was once again flat black.

"Telluria?" she whispered.

From somewhere a in the dark a rumble sounded. The impact of it shook her lungs and made her falter.

Frozen, she tried to control her breathing until a sound like chainmail being dragged across stone hissed into her ears. She screamed, legs pressing down. She got to her feet just as fire bloomed amid a chamber of rune-covered pillars and frescoed walls.

Before the light faded with twisting flickers of orange, a behemoth of a lizard reclined like a bandit prince on a throne of marble slabs and twinkling gems.

The dark came like a cloak, and she was again in the pitch, only the sound of the beast's scales spilling around her. She took a step back, stumbled, and cried out again.

"Quiet!" a voice boomed.

The world shook, and she stifled a scream as she put her hands over her ears and rocked on the moss-covered floor. Moments passed, and as last a subtle flame lit the dark, embers of gold glowing inside the folds of the Dragon's maw.

She looked up, shaking, and saw two huge orange eyes as the massive creature turned his head – as she had no doubt the Wyrm was male. He was shadowed in the subtle light, but she could see he was pale, almost white, with an undertone of crimson that flashed along his scales. Great spire-ridges began on his head and towered up along his spine between two powerful and leather-veined wings. Twin horns drove up from his skull, large enough to pinion an elephant, and great fronds of scaly skin hung from his throat to create a kind of mane, the effect giving him a kingly bearing.

He smelled of brimstone and sky, his breath washing over her enough to make her flesh tingle and sweat.

With a great puff of his nostrils he sucked inward, her hair rising in the intake and she drew further back until he laid a warning claw half the size of her body so close she could make out the pulse beneath the scales attached to it.

"You are of noble blood," he rumbled.

Dumbly, she nodded.

The great orange orb watched her, rolling slowly before the face drew back.

"Disrobe," the beast said.

Blinking, she shook her head, a question tumbling from her lips, "What?"

The Dragon blew a gout of red flame that was touched with blue at its core into the vault, and she screamed again before beginning to pull at her heavy cloaks.

She didn't look up, her fingers trembling as she drew off her over-garments until she stood in only britches, boots, and laced undershirt.

"More," the beast thundered.

At last she raised her chin, sea finally fighting against the beast's fire as she met his gaze.

"Why?" she demanded.

The scales at the back of the Dragon's maw curled and his fire turned from gold to blue and the chamber dimmed.

"I would see my bride in her natural state as she sees me in mine," he answered.

Whatever strength remained to her poured out, and the darkness returned in a comforting nothingness.

CHAPTER THREE

ERIK

A Duke? That is what my title will say. In my youth I knew several Dukes. I looked down on them as a matter of fact, but now I'm going to clutch the title like it was cast into a stormy sea with me.

Why? Igrayn of course, and no matter how I try to convince myself it has some other purpose, surely that is the only reason. Will being a Duke win her? No, but it puts me one step closer to forcing something that she cannot deny, and perhaps it's that show of power that I truly seek.

First, however, I've got to get through this ceremony and then find a way to ChanderNagor. With luck, I can ride by nightfall, but only time and the will of the damnable gods will tell if I will make it on time.

Lady Bianca DeWinter was a vision all in gold. Her dress was polished silk, embroidered with platinum stitching and laced with small pearls about the neck and cuffs at her wrists. She wore a veil of golden lace, and her raven-winged hair was allowed to stream down her back in waves touched here and there with well-placed loops of pearls.

"Lady DeWinter," Maxus bowed.

The golden lady tilted her head slightly at the lord commander's words.

"As Lord Protector of Mahe, I have asked you here in the name of your Lord and Patron, His Majesty Duroban NyWinter, to help in the defense of the city of Mahe and all the people of the West," he continued.

Bianca watched Erik, eyes dark and shaded with ash, before she replied, "As the only remaining blood of the King in this city, I would do as is needed to see to the protection of my people."

The woman's words were honeyed, yet they held the sharp edge of an experienced courtesan.

"My charge is the defense of Mahe, but without noble blood I am a simple dictator, and military rule has never been my goal as an honorable soldier," Maxus continued.

Bianca interrupted, "An honorable soldier is hard to find in such times, Commander, and I thank all the gods that you have been delivered to both me and my people."

Maxus gave a slight bow before he went on. "After much debate, I have found only one solution to this issue, and that is to recreate the Office of the Duke of Mahe."

"I agree, Commander," she replied.

"To fill such an office, I have found the only man of noble blood and battle experience remaining to us in the West. Although his line of kings does not extend to the throne of Aflyr, his ancestors are above reproach.

"Lady, I give to you Prince Erik Fleetwood of Thalonia, and I ask that you give him writ to assume the office as Duke of Mahe and Protector of the West," Maxus concluded.

Bianca's eyes were bright and full of internal flame.

"Sir Fleetwood," she spoke in a clear and honest voice.

Erik stepped forward, his eyes never leaving hers.

"What the Commander has asked here today is not a task without sacrifice. To become the Duke of Mahe you would have to forever renounce your northern titles and swear homage to the defense of Mahe, Aflyr, and the line of NyWinter Kings. Is this still something you wish?" she asked.

Erik bowed to her. "I will serve the people."

"Meaning?" she asked.

He showed only the slightest hint of a smile, "Meaning what we do now is traitorous to the throne of Aflyr and you and I know it. So then I tell you in earnest who will I serve, and it is the people. A better question, perhaps, is whom you serve, Lady DeWinter?"

Eyes narrowing, she bowed her head slightly, whispering, "You know that answer, so let us move on."

He nodded, raising his voice to the collected officers and petty merchants collected in the hall. "My heart and body are already dedicated to you, Lady DeWinter, and the people of this nation. What you ask is not a sacrifice, but a blessing of the gods."

Bianca swept her delicate hand forward and motioned for Erik to kneel. With a fluid motion he complied. From her left a herald stepped forward with a thin blade held with hilt toward her. Taking the sword, she moved it to Erik's shoulder and began her prayer of benediction.

"Nox, the Avenger, God of the Sun, I ask that you witness this anointing. Today I evoke the blood of my ancestors and the will of my people to raise this man to the office of Duke of Mahe. May his sword ever be as just as yours, and may your light ever shine down upon him and his reign in the West."

Tapping Erik from shoulder to shoulder, she then placed the sword back in the grasp of the herald before she continued.

"Rise, Erik Fleetwood, Duke of Mahe and Lord Protector of the West," she proclaimed.

Erik stood and all those around him fell to their knees, last of them the Lady in Gold, her eyes staying with his until the final moment of submission.

"Lady DeWinter," Erik said.

Bianca rose from her bow to meet his gaze.

"The people will be eager to see us both. Will you accompany me to the grand entry, that we may show the people they have not lost their hero, but gained a Duke instead?" he asked offering her his arm.

She took it, the smell of her like honeysuckle as he drew her out to the balcony. Wind struck them like a wave, but they pressed forward, the steel-gray sea churning white in the bay as a throng of several thousand nestled shoulder to shoulder below.

Erik waved a hand and the crowd cheered, Bianca doing the same. Several mermaid banners had been raised, and a joy was alight in the faces.

These people need a leader. They've been far too long under the shadow of the curse and the rulership of the NyWinters.

"They like you," Bianca said.

"They don't know me," he replied.

She turned then, her eyes holding a slight aura of scarlet. Below, the crowd roared into a greater froth, calls amid the throng from a show of visual unity. Slowly, he reached up and unfastened the tie on her veil, the crowd quieting as the wind picked up.

You are certainly a grand fool.

After a long moment, he leaned in and kissed her, the taste sweet and cold until heat from them both rushed up in a shimmering wave. Thunder boomed below, the crowd exploding, and finally he released her from a grasp that had grown tight amid the kiss.

"You overstep," she whispered.

"I am the Duke of Mahe," he replied.

Her eyes fell, "So you are," she said as she departed the balcony. After another wave, Erik followed her, but she was gone, and in the hall he was greeted by those who attended the ceremony, handshakes and suggestions stealing what fire he had from his moment in the limelight.

Erik moved down the hall, the spacious rooms spilling out around him as scented braziers heated the air but left his skin dry. He wore a long green robe, a high-collared coat beneath bearing the smiling mermaid, above crisp, white britches and polished black boots.

So this is what it means to be the Duke of Mahe? Not much different than Erik of Tall Hills, save some spit and polish.

His bedchamber was removed from the other chambers by a small hall, and as he entered the smell of honey'd candles greeted him. Heavy curtains had been drawn over the chamber's two windows, and the bed was turned down with a steaming bowl of water set on the table next to it.

Sighing, he moved inside as a shadow peeled away from a far wall. His hand went for *Fury*, but Bianca drew off her cloaks and he relaxed.

"What is this?" he asked.

"I've come for my kingdom," she replied.

"I don't have time for games, and I should have the guards flogged for letting you in here," he said.

She watched him as he removed his belt and placed *Fury* on a peg next to the bed. After drawing off his robe, he turned back to her and shook his head.

"I'll need sleep, as I'm leaving at first light. This is no place for a lady."

"Is this the way you will have it then?" she asked.

"Have what, exactly?"

Walking a step closer, she let her hand drop to her bodice, a finger trailing over the curve of her breasts.

"You wanted me from the first, and now you can have me," she whispered.

Smiling, he shook his head, "Perhaps that's the reason I no longer want you."

Heat blazed around her, a hand flying freely at his face. He caught it, and she tried the other but it was blocked as well.

"Bastard!"

She struggled against him, and he pushed her until her back stuck heavily against a wall. Air rushed from her lungs in a gasp, and he caught it in his mouth as he covered hers with his. Squirming, clawing, and finally relenting, they joined their heat as clothes were torn asunder.

It was a feral act, sometimes reduced to outright combat and other times sensual and lingering. In the end, they were both wet and spent. She lay atop a tangle of linens, dark hair spilling around her and pale skin aglow in the embers of the braziers still smoldering in the corners.

Erik stood, stretched, and drew a cloth from the basin to wipe his loins. Her smell clung to him even as he threw the cloth back onto the stand and sighed.

She looks like Igrayn lying there in shadow, or at least my mind plays a trick on me as such.

He moved from the chamber, bare feet playing against the cool stone as he drew open a door to the balcony. Outside, a bell chimed from the harbor, but fog clung to the fortress like cheesecloth. He could see little but the marble railing four feet away.

Gooseflesh drew up on his skin, but he moved out and ran his fingers over the dew-slick rail before leaning his weight against it and closing his eyes.

What desire for oblivion follows me? Surely I've lost all hope of finding peace in this land, and now I've plowed another field that I must prey bears no fruit.

"A cold night, no?"

He jumped, hand going to his side but grabbing only air. Naked, he drew back against the rail and searched the mist for the source of the voice, but only grey gloom waited there.

"Show yourself," he hissed.

From the gloom a woman appeared. She was slender, tall, and had a lithe quality that gave her an alien feel beyond common races. Hair golden sunlight, eyes shining like the summer sea, and ears upturned into fine points that gave purchase to the hints of an unearthly beginning.

"Are all Humans to brazen as to go into the winter elements without attire?" she asked.

Her voice pinched her words, and he felt his heat burn her cheeks but kept his hands from covering his loins.

"It was a hot night inside. I came out here to breathe," he replied.

She smiled and his insides twisted. From within her clothing, little more than revealing silks, she withdrew a rod. He eyed the open doorway.

"I am Amilyn, daughter of the Second World. Have no fear, warrior, I've not come to destroy you, but instead to give you help in your current quest," she said.

He raised an eyebrow, "What do you know of my quest?"

"I know that the earth trembles beneath my feet, that the forests quake and the rivers rush, because of the power you have brought into play," she said.

"That isn't an answer."

She moved forward and he held his ground. With a wave of her rod, a shimmer of golden light crept out and touched him. It was cold and yet it burned, but in a flash it was gone and the cold of the night with it. He looked down. He now wore a shining suit of mail. It adorned him like he was a knight of legend.

"These are the gifts I bring, my liege, if you will accept me into you confidence," she said.

Her voice was touched with a hiss, and the hair on the back of his neck stood on end but still he was drawn to her.

"What do your gifts cost?"

His question came out thin, and his breath was caught in wisps of smoke that she drew into her noise and her eyes flared with color.

"I offer you the world and ask nothing in return," she whispered.

Lies... I know they are lies and yet they are sweet like a honey-touched jungle chocolate.

"I leave in the morning," he replied.

"Why wait?" she asked.

With a wave of her rod the mists parted to expose the stables, a boy sleeping in the hay at the entrance and a guard wiping a drip of dew from his helm's nose guard.

"My gifts are many. Just bring me to the war and you will see what I have to offer," she said.

He nodded, moving forward as the guard came to attention.

"Your Grace!? What brings you in this hour?" the guard asked.

The man's eyes went to his armor, growing wide as he passed.

"I need my horse and another," Erik said.

The stable-boy was up and wiping sleep from his eyes as he stumbled away.

"Your Grace, if I might, who is the second horse for?" the guard asked.

Erik turned, but only the mists remained behind him. Shaking his head, he rubbed his gauntleted hands together.

"It doesn't matter, just see it done," he replied.

The guard nodded, and went after the boy, Erik waiting alone in the white, his armor slowly beading up with a thousand drops of water.

CHAPTER FOUR

IGRAYN

The nightmare was there, real, like I could reach out and touch it, but fevered dreams after the attempt on my life are to be expected. No! I must awake, and when I do Nehru will be there like a blessing from the gods.

Igrayn opened her eyes, each blink slow and deliberate. The dark was subtle, a glow like some kind of marsh gas making the green of the moss floor dance in her vision. Above, the darkness was like a pool with the tips of pointed stone falling toward the floor.

She sat up, her heart racing and the sound of the sea rushing in her ears. Behind her the sound of scales hissed and she closed her eyes again.

"I thought the daughter of a king would have more power than what I feel from you," the thunderous voice said.

Swallowing, she drew a breath and opened her eyes again. Her legs stretched out before her, her thighs bare and over-the-knee, black boots adorning their lower half. She looked down, almost gasping as all she saw was a thin strip of black leather bound at her waist and a dark fur cape draped over her shoulders, nothing else.

"What have you done?" she asked.

"Prepared my bride," the Dragon replied.

She turned then, her eyes meeting one orange orb that took her in from across a ten foot divide.

"I am promised by the gods to be the wife of the King of Aflyr," she said.

The Dragon lifted his head, scaly fronds extending from his chin as he provided a toothy smile.

"I don't speak of marriage and Wizard's ceremony. My bride is my guide in this world to stop that which is coming. You are joined to me, much as the Fey will be joined to our enemy, and together we will all decide the fate of this land," he said.

She shook her head, "I don't understand."

"Sometimes, Human, it is not for you to understand. You must simply do. Now stand, and take up the blade so that we might begin the journey before it is too late."

"Blade?" she asked.

The huge orange eye turned and she moved with it until an unsheathed sword came into her line of vision. It was a broadsword, old and with a hilt similar to that of Erik's Fury. She moved over the moss to where it lay.

"It will be heavy," she whispered.

"Only in your mind. Now take it up and let us be away from here."

She touched the hilt and it was cool, the leather worn supple beneath her fingers. Lifting it, her eyes grew wide.

"It has less weight than my sabre," she said.

"And so it would, for my bride, but if you were a warrior twice your size you could not lift it without my blessing on your flesh."

Waving the sword once before her, she asked, "What is this 'Fey'?"

"We are one in the same, two spirits of the world that existed when the gods danced in the fields and no other races called this place home. We are both outsiders, interlopers into the gods' playground, and for that we were punished to be forever linked."

"Like the children's stories," she said.

"Yes, like tales lost in the mists of time, the Fey and the Dragons wander in the shadow until something wakes us and forces our hand."

"Something?"

"Gods... or goddesses mostly, but certainly those with great power, and now the Fey has made her move, and she will try to win favor from a heavenly patron to escape this lamentable prison we both found ourselves in."

Igrayn shook her head. "Where is the Fey now?"

"In the North, with a man who could sway the balance," the Dragon said.

Man? By the gods, has the Fey aligned with King NyWinter?

"We must be away, as the Fey will not wait, and the longer it lays with the Human the better its chance to sway the balance to the side of the goddess."

Her hand trailed down to her bare skin, and she turned back to the Dragon with questioning eyes. He smiled again, and then turned toward the dark, the fires within his mouth lighting the way as he slithered from the chamber.

Telluria, what have you done to me, and what game do the gods play now?

Slowly, holding the sword before her, she followed the creature into the shadow as her boots began to ring against stone.

Ash fell backward, the pony braying as it fled down the ravine. He tumbled into the snow, steam rising as he called to Bandylegs for assistance. Behind him the Dragon crouched, wings outstretched above a rise of stone.

The Eldarin was nimble, rolling and coming up with a handful of flame, but when Igrayn appeared before the beast the blue fire flickered and died away.

"Princess?" he whispered.

She moved down from the height, body sheathed in heat from the beast and her skin as pale as that of the snow around her.

"Ash! I wasn't sure how long I had been away, or if you and Telluria would still be here," she said.

Ash shook his head, copper hair bouncing around his eyes. "Telluria has gone, a day ago, but I was told to remain until…"

She raised an eyebrow, "Until I returned or until it was clear I was never coming back?"

The priest didn't reply. She nodded and walked past him, the Dragon moving down the slope as tumbles of snow drifted back down the ledge and rolled into balls.

"We must go," she said.

Standing, he raced to keep up with her. Steam puffed from his boots in the snow, and his eyes blazed orange like the Dragon that followed them.

"Igrayn, this is insanity! That thing…" he looked back.

The Dragon was creating rivers of water where he walked, the flows breaking down the cliffs in wispy falls.

"He is my mate, and if we are to save Aflyr we must go," she replied.

"Mate!" The priest nearly croaked the word.

She stopped, the sword coming up to shine along its edge from the glow in Ash's eyes.

"Your god is playing here as much as any, priest, and I'll not sate your desire for knowledge other than to say I am still intact…unless the Wyrm has something else to add," she said.

Ash turned from the blade to the Dragon, the orange orbs aglow above him.

"No, no, I see no reason to question this further," he stammered.

Igrayn turned back to the slope, her boots stumbling amid the snow and stones but she felt no cold even in her near-naked state and she kept moving downward. Below, amid the mists and peaks, Nehru lay waiting. She kept her course, Ash right on her heels.

Bells rang in the Nehru tower, and small dark figures ran about the walls as the Dragon blew a great blast of flame skyward. Igrayn, walking the war-torn path toward the main gate, turned back to the beast and scowled. The orange eyes regarded her, and the toothy maw turned into a strange reptilian smile.

"He's not going to make this easy on me," she whispered.

"Bandylegs preserve us," Ash said.

She looked down, the little priest was no taller than her naked hip, but his hair was nearly smoking as he hung near her and watched the men on the walls. From somewhere in the shadows above, a familiar voice called down.

"There is no treasure here for a Wyrm and its dark mistress! Be gone before we launch death down upon you!"

"Rikov doesn't recognize me!" Ash said.

"More like he doesn't recognize me, or is too preoccupied by our new traveling companion to care," she said.

Taking several steps forward, her sword held before her on open palms, she yelled her reply.

"Lieutenant Rikov, it is Igrayn, I've come to pass into the East and ask after our force,"

There was a momentary pause, before the young man called again, "Princess! Has the Wyrm bewitched you?"

She shook her head, "No, Rikov, it has come down from the mountains to help our cause against the Ruks and Delvers. I don't ask you open the fortress to us, but that you tell me of Erik and the rest of our company."

Another long pause, then she could see Rikov's form appear full on the battlements.

"Gone, Princess, the hillmen left with the Kin yesterday by way only the mountain folk know bound for the North, and Erik was gone before you left with Telluria days ago."

Erik was gone?

"Where did Sir Tall Hills go?" she called.

"No one knows, save that he didn't leave by the main gate, and Captain Braxus said no more on the subject save that he was gone."

"Where would he go?" Ash asked.

She looked down and shook her head, "I don't know, but I fear I may have been the cause."

"You?"

Nodding, she looked back up at Rikov, "We will go to the East. It is the only way we know to go, and it will be faster for the Dragon. Has Telluria returned?"

"No, we've not seen the Wizard since she left with you. Our scouts report that the Delvers are clear in the southeast, their path of destruction leaving no means of supply and their course bound for ChanderNagor," Rikov answered.

"Are you seriously thinking of following a Delver army north…all by yourself?" Ash asked.

She smiled, "Well, we do have a Dragon."

"And me," a voice called from a fallen defensive work.

They turned, as Tavalori appeared from the shadows with his bow in hand. To Igrayn's right, Ash's heat bloomed to new highs.

"You didn't go with the army?" Igrayn asked.

The ranger shook his head, "No, I waited for you, since you slipped out of the fortress without telling me."

Her cheeks took on a shade of red, but she lowered her sword and nodded, "It was Telluria."

"I figured," he replied.

Behind them the Dragon roared and the ground trembled. The beast moved forward, pebbles bouncing on the snowy road as it did.

"The Goddess plays again," it boomed.

Fire leaked in dripping hisses from its mouth, and Tavalori backed up with bow at the ready. Igrayn stepped before the charging wyrm, her sword in hand.

"What are you doing!" she demanded.

The Dragon pulled up short, but its eyes never left the young ranger.

"You would protect our enemy?" it asked.

"Tavalori is my protector," she replied.

"In fairness, he doesn't have a very good record on that front," Ash whispered.

"Shhhh!" she hissed, then lowered the blade, "I've taken much of what you've said on faith, but in this I must go with what I know to be true."

The Dragon blew another blast of blue flame skyward but backed away, rumbling, "Do as you will, but remember the gift I would have given when this thing turns on you."

Igrayn's arms were shaking, but she took a long breath and then looked back to Tavalori. The young man stood pale in the dim light beneath steely clouds, his hood drawn and his long handsome face covered with a thin stubble of blond growth at the chin.

Would you really betray me?

"Thank you," he said, "You won't regret it."

She nodded.

I hope that is true.

CHAPTER FIVE

ERIK

What gifts have been bestowed on me in this fashion? What charms have been laid that I cannot see? These are things that spin in my head like webs so thick I can't see through them.

There were times, when I was in the Planar Archipelago, that I knew of power – or enchantments and magic – beyond the realms of our common Wizards. Shera warned me of such things, shielded me from their power because at my heart I am a man who wants to be found desirable by beauty beyond this world.

So I now go into this oblivion, but there is a part of me who holds back still, a part that still speaks to you, Lurker. Perhaps it is not my destiny yet to be drawn away, but only time will tell if I have the strength to overcome these pitfalls that await my impassioned desires.

The day drifted overhead beneath spotted clouds as Erik guided SmokeShadow down the lonely road toward Ixprys. Behind him, a second horse was tethered, but the Fey rode instead against his back, her arms wrapped low on his waist and her head resting against his plated shoulder.

"We make poor time riding like this," he said.

She tightened her grip, fingers dangerously close to his loins. "War will wait, my warrior, and you have a head start on your force waiting at Ixprys."

"How do you know that?"

"I am of the world, I feel its flow like the tide, and I know what awaits us in the East," she replied.

"You sound like a seer, and I don't trust seers," he said.

"I have no powers over prophecy or the future, but where men walk is known to me. Lay your worry aside, and take pleasure in what I have to offer."

"And what exactly is that, save a suit of armor?"

She laughed, the sound like tinkling crystal in his ear. "I would offer you everything, if you would only take it."

"Again, that isn't an answer."

"Oh, but it is, even if it is one you don't trust."

He shook his head, "Should I really trust a woman who appears from the mist to grant me boons, and then sweeps me out of the palace in the middle of the night?"

"It is certainly not the first bed you've left before sunrise," she observed.

"Again, you speak as though you are a seer."

"I simply understand the man I have been sent to," she replied.

"Ah, and now we get somewhere!"

She sighed, and he continued, "So who exactly sent you?"

"The floor of the world brought me to you," she answered.

"No, that is a lie," he said.

She pulled away, and he looked over his shoulder at her. The beauty of her face was masked for a moment in the shadow of a cloud, but she smiled nonetheless.

"Now you are the seer, knowing my heart and purpose?" she asked.

"I am a man trained by a master rogue, and I can read people better than most," he said.

"Master Rogue? Do tell."

He shook his head, "You deflect, and I'll not play your game."

Leaning back to rest on his back, she whispered, "But my games can be the most fun."

"Let's just get to Ixprys, then I can decide what to do with you," he said.

"As you wish, my warrior, but that battlefield is still miles away."

He shook his head. *Battlefield? She's playing again, but the longer I'm with her, the harder it is to think straight. Shera, if only you were here you'd set this straight! But now I've got to depend on myself.*

They road on, the skeletal trees and a few dusky sparrows their only company as the shadows of the late season day grew long.

Frost lay heavy on the deep grass, the trees bare and the shelter no more than a heavy blanket and a few hewn sticks. Erik lay beneath, his fire chilled, with the Fey next to him in her silks and sweet smells. Her blond hair fell down under his chin, and she clung to him as though she were a spent lover instead of a simple traveling companion.

Outside, SmokeShadow clomped amid the morning light that came in great golden towers down from the heavy clouds. The rays turned the world to glittering diamond, and with a great sigh, Erik pushed himself free of the Fey's embrace and ran his tongue over his front teeth.

White breath smoked out on his exhale, and the Fey stirred, her eyes fluttering open and her smile locking his heart in a tight grip.

"A fair morning, my Master," she said.

He nodded and tried to leave the shelter, but her hands held his shoulder as she leaned in and ran her lips along the base of his neck.

"Must you resist me even when we have such a beautiful morning to share?" she whispered.

Heat bloomed between them, and he closed his eyes.

"We must be away. The forces are mustering," he said.

"They can wait, as you lead them," she said.

She kissed him again, and he turned to her, his lips finding hers as he fell back, the weight of her body unusually light as she pressed him downward. Her hand pulled at the ties of his armor, pieces coming loose like tiles from a roof in a gale wind. There was no spark in her, not the fire of Bianca or the water of Igrayn, just the intoxication of her breath and the pull it put on his eyelids.

Whatever warmth he created was sucked away into her waiting mouth, and the shimmer of the morning light dimmed.

"Come with me, find peace in my womb, warrior, and you will know what bliss is for all eternity," she whispered.

His muscles strained against her, but she pressed down and moaned as he finally entered her. Only grey remained in his vision, and his breath slowed with each rocking movement as she cast her hair down about his face.

"You will sleep, and the Second World will be your new home," she continued.

Her lips found his, cold like ice, and she clawed into his chest, her nails plowing lines of numbness down his skin.

Is this my end? It would be fitting, to die in the pursuit of one desire I could never control.

With a flash, light washed over them and the beauty of the Fey above him became distorted and foreign, her eyes shining black and her skin a sickly grey-green. She screamed, her body convulsing as she fell off him and he sluggishly rolled to the side.

Wind tore through the shelter ripping the blanket away, and daylight streamed in as Erik struggled to his feet. His head pounded and he coughed bile. Struggling, he found a sapling and clung to it like a drowning sailor. Shielding his eyes, he strained to look beyond the edge of the meager camp.

"Telluria?" he stammered.

The Wizard stood tall in white and gold, sun streaming around her as her staff blazed with azure flame. The Fey was up now, but Telluria held out her staff and light burst from the twin blades, striking out and bathing the creature in flame. The Fey's beauty was stripped away until an alien thing stood screaming and clawing at the flickering magic around it.

Erik blinked, the light clearing his mind as he saw *Fury* hanging from a scabbard at Telluria's waist. He rushed forward, drew the blade and turned on the Fey. The creature had fallen back, knees buckled and arms raised against the light. He took three steps forward and brought the sword up but Telluria's voice called a halt.

"No! She is a key, if even a dark one, and her death will cost us everything."

He turned back to the Wizard, *Fury* lowering as he regarded her.

"She has bewitched me," he hissed.

Telluria looked down, her eyes lingering a moment on his naked loins, and the smell of the sea overwhelmed the camp.

"I see that, Your Grace, but that doesn't change what is to be."

"And what is that?" he asked.

"The Fey is only half of the equation, the darkness to the light, and if we kill her both sides will disappear."

"Then what would you do?"

Telluria looked back at the Fey, staff still raised and blazing light. "I will return her to her slumber, if it is within my power to do so. Even still you will have to be wary."

He nodded, and looked back at the creature, its mortal beauty returning slightly as its eyes became human once more. Fingers white at the knuckle, he stepped closer as Telluria's light shifted and spun around them.

The Fey cursed and spat, black bile dribbling from its mouth until a spasm ripped through it as it fell full on the frozen ground. Heat bloomed, and the frost turned to small rivers amid the brown grass, the tender fronds growing as they wrapped themselves around the creature. Beside her, the rod the Fey employed to create his armor shifted, the metal and gems transforming into a twisting staff tipped with firebirds.

The Fey continued to struggle, and the hairs on the back of Erik's neck stood on end as he watched the earth reclaim the creature, pulling her beneath the brown soil. At last the light subsided, and he turned back to Telluria just as she collapsed, a trickle of blood dripping crimson from her thin nose.

He caught her, dropping *Fury* in the process, and turned her over to rest in his lap as he knelt on the warm ground.

"Telluria?" he whispered.

Her eyes fluttered, and he wiped the blood with his fingers.

"It is done, but her power was more than I thought possible," she said.

"What can I do?" he asked.

"Leave me, go to Ixprys and meet your army Your Grace. The path is now clear to do what must be done," she whispered.

He shook his head, "No."

She sighed and closed her eyes, lips moving but no words coming out. He reached up, brushed wet hair from her face and then looked back to his broken shelter.

I will not abandon those who save my life, no matter what service the world may decide it needs from me.

Laying her gently on the grass, he went about recreating his camp, the daylight warm even in the chill of mid-winter. When he came to the staff, he avoided it, walking around the item twice before it disappeared. He spun several times looking for it, but it was gone, just as the Fey had vanished, and he shrugged his shoulders.

Let whatever magic brought her return with her, for this world is a better place with her in it.

"You were foolish to stay," Telluria said.

The fire crackled between them, the light of the Ghost Moon obscured by heavy clouds and wisps of snow dribbling into the light before succumbing to the flame.

"You were foolish to try to send me away," he replied.

A smile crept over her lips until she bit down and stopped it. He offered her a slice of cheese and she took it, nibbling as he sliced triangular bits of bread from a hard loaf.

"How did you know where I'd be?" he asked.

"The magic. It was disturbed by the coming of the two, and once I found my way to Mahe it was easy to follow her scent."

He nodded, adding, "I know how I got to Mahe, but I have to wonder how you did so."

"We all have our secrets, no?"

"True enough, but I have to ask, if the darkness befell me in Mahe, then what about the light?" he asked.

Telluria didn't reply, just chewed on her cheese until he offered her another piece of bread.

"It's not like you to hold something back," he said.

"There are powers at play that I don't understand, and speaking conjecture about them might tip a balance I'm not prepared to be involved in," she replied.

He smiled, "Conjecture works for me."

"You ask after things best left alone," she said.

"I would know what you have to say."

She didn't reply, just sat warming her hands as the fire crackled. Finally, he looked away and sighed.

"Well, whatever the case, at least the South is safe, and Igrayn with it," he said.

Telluria nodded, the smell of the ocean drifting into the camp.

Lying again. It's becoming a habit for women to lie to me, and that isn't good.

"Can you tell me of her?" he asked.

Telluria looked up, her face a mask of calm.

"She's dead," she whispered.

He leaned forward, heart thumping in his chest, and heat rising like a bonfire. Telluria, her water pressed back, fell away.

His voice was a hiss, and he had trouble hearing with the blood in his ears, "What?"

"She was taken by the light. It was the only way," she said.

The fire inside ebbed and fell away, the cold closing in as he sat numbly back on the blankets beneath him.

"Why didn't you tell me this sooner?" he asked.

"I knew the blow would be great, and I had hoped to get through the coming battle first," she said.

Battle? What does the battle matter now?

"What will you do?" she asked.

He shook his head.

"Without Igrayn you are free, the Fey is no more threat, and the paths you might have travelled before meeting us are open to you," she continued.

Blinking, he looked across the fire at her. She was pale as the snow, hair dark like the raven's wing, and there was not a wrinkle of other sign of age on her features.

I should leave, do as I was supposed to when this all began and find my way north to Findalynn or Bandar Abbas.

"Tell me, Duke of Mahe, Your Grace, what will you do?"

She was smiling, if only slightly, and an azure shade set about her cheekbones as the sea rolled in.

Duke of Mahe... yes, I am that, even if just as some great joke. Whatever I am, I'm no coward, and I'll live to my responsibility to these people if even just to get them past this threat.

"I have a secret of my own," he said.

"I'm sure more than one," she replied.

"It's good the duel with the Fey didn't cost you your sense of humor. Be that as it may, we should have company tomorrow," he said.

"Company?"

"Yes, the priest Todmann was sent from Mahe with two thousand foot and a relief company of lancers to hold the roads west of Ixprys. He left five in days before I arrived in Mahe. With them already in play..."

"Your combined force from Nehru should be enough to break a siege on ChanderNagor," she finished.

"That is the plan, assuming Braxus has made it to Ixprys before me and that Cronin and Sire FreeAxe have collected more strength in the inlands."

"Then you will stay?" she asked.

"I do not break contracts easily, a lesson from my old master," he answered.

There was a moment's pause, the snow petering out and Erik throwing another stick on the fire before Telluria spoke. "You should be proud, Erik, for what you have done for this country, for Igrayn, and for the Legion."

He shook his head, "You give me too much credit."

"No, you give yourself too little. No matter what drives you, some purpose deep down keeps your course true to an honorable path, even if it serves your more...base...desires," she said.

He looked at her, the smile hanging half fulfilled, "Thanks...I think."

She sighed, and rose to her feet. "I need to walk, feel the Afterglow around me from the connection to the water in the snow. Get some sleep if you can, I will wake you when morning comes."

He watched her go, the white robes she wore almost blending with the snow where she walked. He shook his head when he saw her boots lying discarded next to his shelter.

I will never understand Wizards or any water-born, and I will never see Igrayn again for whatever fate I thought might have had in store for us is broken.

Finding his blanket, he fell into the shelter, thoughts of the Fey, the war, and Igrayn keeping him awake until the fire burned down to embers and the Blood Moon surpassed her sister in the sky.

CHAPTER SIX

IGRAYN

*O*f all the possible dreams I had as a girl of becoming a wife, having a Dragon bound to me was not one of them. My mother used to say I was special, but then again she said the same of my brother and he was little more than a royal breeding hound.

When I think about the days I spent, the years, of my youth in Sastrine, it makes me wonder what happened to make this moment more real. It is almost as if my past is the tale told about fairies, and the joining with the Dragon is a common thing – like drinking or drawing a breath.

As I move through a landscape filled with burned farms and ruined towns, I have to wonder why I ever left the secluded shores of my homeland. This time away was meant to be my last escape, a chance to find myself, to live free, and find some physical solace, but instead I've found only war, death, frustration…and a mate.

Tavalori is still here, always beside me unless Ash is there with his coy looks and fevered temperatures. The Dragon is no help, whatever grudge he carries against Tavalori making each day more uncomfortable than the last.

I also have no idea where we are going or what we will find when we get there. Tavalori leads us, but the Dragon calls halts, direction changes, and strange nature communions before we continue ever north.

Whatever the future holds, I wonder why Erik is more commonly in my thoughts than the young man beside me in the flesh.

"What is it?" Ash asked.

The pit was little more than a gash in the center of the town, cobbles tossed aside and a large rust stain permeating the center.

"A ceremony," the Dragon rumbled.

The priest turned to look up at the head looming over him. "Ceremony for what?"

"Something was summoned here, something not of this world," the Dragon answered.

Igrayn's skin prickled and she ran her hands over her forearms. Around her, buildings tumbled down, bodies lay frozen in light snow, and blackened timbers sprouted from rooftops. Wind blew black ash into a grey conflagration amid the snow.

"If something was brought into being here, was it the darkness you spoke of?" Igrayn asked.

The Dragon swung its head from side to side, "No, that darkness has been put to sleep. The threat has been eliminated for the moment."

She turned, "Will that mean you will leave as well?" she asked.

"As long as I am bound to you, I may remain, but my power will dwindle without its other half present in this world."

"What is he talking about?" Ash asked.

Igrayn shook her head, "Dragon and Fey are joined in some way, and one cannot exist without the other. If the Fey is abed, then the Dragon will need to return to its torpor as well."

"A Fey? Aren't they enchantresses, creatures who take men to their earthy homes and keep them like flies trapped in amber?" Ash asked.

She regarded him, and the Dragon blew flame into the air before saying, "The priest knows the tales of old, more than you, my mate."

"Then if the Fey is asleep, King NyWinter must have been taken or has found a way to defeat her," Igrayn said.

"Assuming King NyWinter was the target," Tavalori added.

Wind swept around her, and the furs opened to expose her enough that Ash turned away and Tavalori gaped.

"If not King NyWinter, then who?" she asked.

"Whoever has a better change to stop the creature summoned and keep this nation from falling into oblivion," the Dragon said.

"Erik…" she whispered.

"What?" Tavalori asked.

She shook her head, "Nothing, we should find a place to sleep the night."

Tavalori nodded, and moved away, Ash taking up as position next to her, the Dragon moving into a half-burned building with its scales crushing timbers like straw.

"You should put Erik from your mind," Ash said.

Igrayn nodded. *I will, and what better way to do it than with Tavalori. If the Fey has taken Erik, then what else is there to hold me back?*

Igrayn's palm hadn't even touched the door handle to her appropriated room in the abandoned farmhouse, when the portal was thrown open and Tavalori pulled her inside. His lips found hers, and the door slammed behind them as he tore at her fur cloak. There was a moment of struggle, but she relented, the smell of the sea rising.

Igrayn fumbled with his shirt, her fingers tearing at the laces and then pulling upward at the waist until the linen was lifted over his arms revealing his smooth skin beneath. He kissed her again as they spun about the room, each turn removing another piece of his clothing. Their mouths tried desperately to devour one another, and she let out a whimper as he pulled away and bit at her neck.

Their course led them to a small bed covered with a single torn blanket, and, with a final act of power, Tavalori spun her down with his weight following into her.

As her naked back struck the fabric the air around them exploded in a shower of white powder. Tavalori choked and tears welled in Igrayn's eyes as they each inhaled the white dust, the remainder of the cloud bathing their skin and filling the room in a kind of fog.

Both of them struggled to stand, skin flushing red and convulsions shaking their chests. They choked and gagged on the powder, and Igrayn's tongue swelled as her eyes puffed and ran. She staggered forward to a chair and managed to throw her cloak back over her near-naked body.

Tavalori stumbled, his britches down around his ankles as he moved to the door. She coughed behind him until he managed to open the door, the two of them escaping into the pure air of the hall in a fit of scratches and rasps.

Igrayn blinked back tears, and Tavalori struggled to get his pants back around his waist.

"How?" Tavalori choked.

Igrayn shook her head just as the small form of Ash came bounding up the steps with his breath ragged and his face flushed. A wave of heat followed him, and she whispered curses between coughs as his mustache hid the hint of a grin.

You little bastard! I'll see you pay for this damnable game...

"Igrayn... Tavalori, are you injured?" Ash asked.

Igrayn waved him back, her eyes red and her heart pounding.

"It looks like the Ruks must have left traps about this place," Ash continued, "but lucky for you both, Bandylegs had me warm snow for a bath in a tub I found in the winter-garden below."

"You..." Tavalori said before more coughs ripped from his throat.

Around the ranger there was a haze of darkness, something foreign, and for the first time the corruption of his element was palpable.

By the Goddess! Could the Dragon have been right?

"Come, I'll get you to the bath, and when Tavalori is recovered enough, he can use it after," Ash said.

The priest took her hand, and she didn't resist. Her eyes fell on those of Tavalori for a moment. His mouth quivered in response with a thousand words unspoken. Looking away, she pulled the cloak closer around her and stifled a shudder.

When the two were out of earshot, Ash looked back, whispering, "Did you feel that?"

She nodded.

"Erik said once that he felt Tavalori's spark was 'off' and only now do I understand what he meant," Ash continued.

"Perhaps that Ruk trap was more a favor than a betrayal," she said.

"Well, Bandylegs works in mysterious ways," Ash replied.

She stopped, "Then you are admitting it was Bandyleg's doing?"

He smiled up at her, his heat turning her cheeks rosy, "I'm saying one can never understand the will of a god, but I've put my faith in his wisdom, no matter how strange it might seem."

Shaking her head, she pushed past him, another round of coughs following her down the stairs.

Tavalori followed at a distance, his cloak drawn up and his eyes shielded. Igrayn felt him as much as saw him. Whatever had changed in his nature with the final denial of their coupling was now a scent on the wind that threatened to gag her.

Ash was next to her, his heat a welcome feeling even with her water stirring at the proximity. The Dragon, for its part, had slowed, and she looked back as it lagged a hundred feet behind Tavalori amid the ragged pines of the eastern inlands.

"He grows weaker," she said.

Ash looked back. "I know. His fire has dimmed, and yet he moves on tirelessly as though there is an end that matters when this journey comes to a close."

"Do *you* think that there will be an end that matters?" she asked.

He smiled, "Bandylegs wouldn't lead me this way if there wasn't."

"I guess what matters doesn't have to mean a happy ending," she said.

"That may be true, but at least the Dragon is on our side, and the Fey has been taken out of play."

"That doesn't help us with whatever was summoned back at the village," she added.

Ash rubbed his hands together and brought steam forth in the cold air. "You may be right there, and whatever summoned that was no Wizard, so I fear there is another god in play."

"Who would have such a connection? The Jackal?" she asked.

"Could be, but Ruks don't worship that god. Perhaps only the Delvers do, and I think it would be hard to mix leaders of the army with something they fight against. Remember, Ruks turned their back on the Jackal when their brethren the Delvers fell to his power."

"Then who?"

"If I had to assume? My faith thinks it might be Lovillis," he answered.

Igrayn pulled her cloak around her, something on the wind taking the name and stretching it into a haunting note.

"What would the Arcanian Goddess of Suffering have to do with this?" she asked.

"I cannot say, but one of her priestesses could make the summoning if she had the appropriate sacrifices. The town could have provided that."

Dark pacts, a nation across the sea, and now demons. What hope have I of ever having some thread of happiness?

"Whatever the case, we've only got another day till we slip across the northern roads to Ixprys, and there we might learn the fate of our friends," he finished.

And the fate of Erik, assuming he's even there.

CHAPTER SEVEN

ERIK

War, it is coming and a part of it is of my making. I chose to do this. I wanted it because I wanted to cheat fate, play dice against the Gods, and break laws that were unbreakable. Is that pride? Is it insanity?

Perhaps it is both, I cannot say. Whatever the case, I now lead a force to the East into the waiting maw of death and my motivation for doing so is dead.

"A rider approaches," Telluria said.

Erik looked up the road until he saw the mounted knight moving along a line of pine trees toward their current position. Behind him, Todmann's force marched in step, and a small collection of officers, and the Wizard, rode with him at the front.

"I believe its Gariaus," she added.

He nodded, the banner on the man's lancer standing out against the green of the trees.

"He was with Braxus, which means the army must have made it through," he said.

Todmann broke in from Erik's right, "Then let's hope he brings fortuitous news."

Erik nodded, the sounds of his new lances and infantry clanking away on the road behind him.

Two thousand foot and another two-hundred and fifty lance. I hope it will be enough.

Gariaus's horse was covered in foam, and his clothes were dirty and near frozen to him as he pulled up short of the lead lancers and asked to see Erik.

With a wave, Erik released his outriders and they brought the man up as he provided a hasty salute.

"Your Grace, I have word from Captain Braxus," the man spoke, his voice raspy and dry.

Erik pulled SmokeShadow closer and leaned in so that those around him couldn't hear the report.

"Braxus sent me to find you, hoping you'd be on the march," Gariaus said.

"Well, you've found me. So what is your report?"

"Yes, my apologies Your Grace. The Captain has taken his force west of Ixprys and our scouts reported a battlefield on the road to Mahe half a day from the crossroads. He awaits your force before going any further."

Erik nodded. *A good man, Braxus, and wise not to engage without proper support in case the enemy holds the city.*

"Your Grace?" prompted another of his Captains, his only female commander, Caelie Bloodstar, who had come up from the ranks of lances.

Erik raised a gloved hand to quiet her, returning his focus to the exhausted rider.

"Gariaus, find a fresh horse among the Lances, we'll take a half-hour rest and then return to the road. Can you ride with us?" Erik asked.

"Your Grace!" the man saluted.

"And, Gariaus, your news has been delivered, and, as Duke, I would have no one in the procession know of it." Erik added.

Around Erik the Captains waited, their faces taut and concerned. He looked from them back up the line until his eyes met those of Telluria who had fallen back from the command company. He nodded at her, a wan smile on his lips.

"The way to Ixprys is clear. Captain Bloodstar, send the word among the troops, but have them know that the city of may be under siege. We will have a short rest and then move on as we must increase our speed if we are to assist the king," he ordered.

She relaxed at the words before turning to the heralds and issuing the orders. In a matter of minutes the footman had settled in, and Telluria and Todmann remained horsed and next to him.

"Is there anything else?" the priest asked.

"A battle has taken place, but Braxus holds his force back from it. We will know more the closer we get," Erik answered.

"The end is near," Telluria said.

Erik smelled the ocean, deep and cold, but he didn't reply, instead spurring SmokeShadow on up the road.

This will not be the end for me. I don't give in that easily. Even if the world seems darker now there are always reasons to live.

Thank the Gods for the cold.

Erik watched the battlefield as his men moved slowly through it. The litter of dismembered bodies was laid out all around them, a feast for carrion birds and other scavengers.

The enemy spared nothing from its fury, the knights and men-at-arms butchered alongside the women, children, and even the livestock of this unfortunate wagon train.

"Who were they?" asked Cronin, his fur-covered shoulders laced with snow.

Erik looked down along the wagon column before shouting for scouts to seek out any banners, standards, or tabards among the ruin.

"From the look of them, I'd say we had ourselves a great deal of nobility here, probably Mahe born," Braxus replied.

Much of the dead were naked, and larger scavenging animals had spread the remains about the field as though the battle was weeks old.

Erik nodded, "Agreed, and Ixprys has no nobility like this. It's a river town well placed to the north of the inlands, and it's at the crossroads of the east and west of Aflyr, but it is not affluent."

"Could this be the remains of those who fled Mahe at the call of the King a month ago?" Telluria asked.

Braxus shook his head, "Let's hope not. Both our force and that of the King would be a might screwed if this was the host he called to his banner from Mahe."

Cronin nodded and then moved away, barking out orders to his improvised army to recover anything of value.

Erik sat atop his steed and waited, his eyes searching the remains of the field around him as the wind blew a fresh dusting of snow over the carnage.

There would have been over three thousand souls in the train, many of those knights. No rag-tag raider band like we've discovered in the south coast could have done this.

"Your Grace" one of his few remaining assigned lancers called as he wheeled his mare around the wreckage of a wagon to come alongside him. The young knight produced a piece of cloth.

Reaching out, Erik took a piece of a standard and stared at it a long moment.

"Mahe regular..." he said to himself.

"Your Grace," the lancer confirmed.

Erik shook his head.

The King was already in trouble without the Knights from Nehru, but without the support of the might of Mahe, his fate grows even dimmer. If a battle was to take place at ChanderNagor, it would be a vicious test of the king's ability to lead his troops against a host as strong as any seen in the Old Kingdoms for hundreds of years.

Looking back down at the bodies, the tell-tale sign of Jai-Ruk Cleavers and the broken, red-shafted arrows of low Delver archers showed the breadth of the slaughter.

This was an army of the Broken Land, and it had come to destroy everything in its path, of that there can be no doubt.

"Orders, Your Grace?" the lancer interrupted his line of thought.

Grim-faced, Erik answered, "Send our best scouts forward to Ixprys, but tell them that we must have news of the town. They are not to risk themselves in combat."

"Your Grace!" the lancer responded with a salute.

Erik reached out and caught the man by the arm, adding, "And send a rider to Mahe. They must know about this and the threat that looms if we fail."

The lancer's face was pale but he saluted again and then rode off looking for his remaining riders.

Sitting on his horse a moment longer, he finally slipped from the saddle and started helping with the recovery. In this climate his men would need wood for fires, and the fallen wagons would make for good shelter should they learn that Ixprys had fallen to the same fate as this host of Mahe.

The Cursed Legion of Mahe made the march to Ixprys in just under eight hours, with riders moving back and forth constantly among Erik, Sire FreeAxe, and Braxus.. When they reached the half burned river town it was an empty shell. No bodies, no sign of combat, and no resources were left among the abounded buildings.

The men were on a six-hour rest, just enough for sleep and a cold meal in the face of another light snow-shower before they would again return to the road. Erik sat with his command staff in a tavern overlooking the river, the windows shaded with leather blankets as the panes were shattered, and candles burning around the table. They'd managed some warm wine and trail rations, each of them taking their part as the tallows burned down.

"It'll be a nar good thing we find in ChanderNagor," Cronin spoke over his flagon of warmed wine.

Erik did not reply, the rest of his commanders nodding their agreement. Around him in the common room were those he trusted in combat: Braxus, Malcolm, Cronin, Sire FreeAxe, Telluria, and Caelie Bloodstar – the battle-scarred and yet remarkably attractive young Captain from the Legion Lancers he had taken a liking to. Todmann was ministering to the troops, some men suffering the effects of the adverse weather.

"Our scouts have witnessed some rogue Delvers in the field country between here and ChanderNagor, but those were dispatched without incident," Bloodstar offered.

FreeAxe drank deeply, adding, "Then it must be assumed that the Delver force that destroyed this Mahe wagon train believes its rear free of any enemy."

"Then we should strike quickly." Braxus said.

"Agreed," Malcolm nodded, the mercenary having recovered from his wounds at Tall Hills.

Telluria watched, her green eyes taking in everything. Erik caught himself staring at her and shook his head to clear it.

"We will move in force to ChanderNagor, but until we know the lay of the land, the current tide of battle, and the numbers we face, we can make no other determination. This means we stay to the woods, stay out of direct sight, and hide our advance as long as possible," Erik said.

FreeAxe grunted, and the others gave their support, all but Telluria. "Wouldn't it prove better to show our force, make the Delver army adjust to our advance, and help free up the King to recover before the conflict grows?"

"I've never faced a battle in which my direct presence helped me defeat an enemy. We will stick with stealth," Erik replied.

The Wizard watched him, and their sparks collided making the air moist and warm over the table, the rest of the company finding other places to rest their eyes.

You play, Telluria, and you are wise enough to see my true motivations aren't you?

"When the sun comes up, I want the army already on the road. Malcolm, you will take command of the First Mahe Footmen, and Braxus you will have the Second. That is two thousand men between you. Do you think you can handle that?" Erik asked.

The mercenaries smiled and Erik nodded as he turned to Bloodstar. "You will be with me and the lancers. Understood?"

"Yes, Your Grace," she answered without hesitation.

"Sire FreeAxe, could you bring your Kin up in the reserve as we march along with the hillmen under Cronin's command?" he asked.

FreeAxe raised his tankard, "Let the fire blaze the trail, we of earth will be ready when the call comes from the trumpets."

Cronin smiled, his dark eyes aglow as he and the Kin drank and thickened the air with their combined spark.

"And what of me?" Telluria asked.

"You will go with Malcolm. I don't want a repeat of what happened at Tall Hills," Erik answered.

She tightened her lips, but nodded.

I'll need you, certainly, but right now I need my own course laid without interference or conscience.

"Commanders," Erik said, sliding his chair from the table and standing with a slight bow. Around him, the rest of the commanders moved to their feet as well. They saluted him, and then exited swiftly, each with his own agenda to be seen to before the coming dawn.

The road was growing ever shorter, and within another two days all these brave warriors' destinies would be played out, no matter what path I might choose after we get there.

Erik sat in the darkness of his room, the cold air misting his breath and the sound of the wind flapping against the shutters.

He sighed and slipped his hand from the covers to his left ear. His fingers touched the small gold loop of his single earring before pulling it from the lobe.

In the instant the gold ring left his ear it shifted until it reshaped into a circlet of dull fabric, thin runes running around the well-worn length. With a smile, he flipped item between his hands, his thoughts drifting back to the time where he had found it.

Where are you Shera? Do you even know of this war, or would you even care? When I found this item, you made sure it would be left to me to use it wisely. A Shaper's Charm can be used to make its owner almost anything, and with it I could slip away just as I did in Taux when the Druid's Rangers caught my trail.

Placing the circlet on his head, it shrunk and scuttled like an insect back to his ear, where it was once again a shining, gold loop.

If that weren't easy enough, the Pegasi Rod is still mine to use. In a flash I could be home, wherever I chose that place to be.

Rolling in the covers, he watched the crimson light of the Blood Moon trace a line across the floor near the bed.

Igrayn is dead, and for some reason I can't seem to get over that. We weren't a couple, far from it, but by the gods she was inside my head and I fear my heart. Now I feel like I've lost a chance that could have been great...

Shera, you'd tell me to follow my instincts, as was your way, but I'm not bound by the eternal lifespan of air, pulling me wherever the wind takes me. No, I've got only a handful of years, and when a chance is missed for a Human there is no certainty that it will come round again.

Outside a horse patrol passed and he pulled the cover up further over his head, the cold chilling his ears and nose.

Still, things were so much simpler on in the Planar Archipelago, where you were always my guide. Now, I've got to make all the decisions myself and they weigh heavier by the day. My freedom evaporates like dew on the morning, and unless I leave right now, this trap will close and it will be too late.

Closing his eyes, he caught flashes of Igrayn's face on the night he'd saved her from the demon of the Mahe Palace. She was so young, fresh, and innocent as she nuzzled against him.

In that moment, I could have held her forever, so unlike Bianca who now waits for me in Mahe with the promise of political marriage and the burdens that come with it.

"Your Grace?" a guard's voice spoke from outside the door.

Erik sighed, his eyes pressing tight before finally opening.

"Yes?"

"Two outriders have returned. They have news of ChanderNagor," the guard replied.

No leaving now, what's done is done, and I will have to see it through to whatever end it takes me.

"Give me ten minutes and then send them in," Erik ordered.

"Your Grace," the man confirmed.

Erik got to his feet and stretched, coughed, and began to dress.

If there was ever a time to bring me luck, my goddess, I need it today.

CHAPTER EIGHT

RELAN

Power comes like the ebb and flow of a great ocean, and when the power of the Fey faded, the flow reversed into me once more. Certainly my journey from the Second World took longer than I'd hoped, and even when the Phoenix Staff returned, the dark paths were unclear, but finally I walk among the frozen fields once more.

Now I must find the battle, and the agents of the goddess that have brought it about. If the Fey was forced back into her slumber, than a Wizard surely plays at the game as well, or the Dragon was much more powerful than I'd anticipated.

Whatever the case, I have a long road ahead, and what I find at the end of it will place more blood upon my hands.

An army marched to the south, the shining pikes and bright helms catching the rays of the morning sun. Relan watched them from afar, his vision enhanced by the power of the Oak Father and his hands wrapped tightly around his staff.

They are the forces of Mahe, going to war for the King in ChanderNagor.

At the head of the column road a company of knights, one in armor that shone with elemental magic. Beside him the white and gold robes of a Wizard the Order of Towers. She was tall, almost as tall as the shining knight, and her hair was black at the temple and nearly violet as it spilled down her back.

You have been blessed by the power of the staff, knight, that armor a gift from the Fey before she was forced from the world.

There was a Kin Sire upon a heavy pony with them as well, the power of his earth laying like a cloud around the group as they road. There were Inlanders with them too, earth-touched Humans. But there was no Wyrm; the other half of the twins nowhere to be found.

He raised his face to the wind, the breeze carrying with it the corruption of the Planes and the failing scent of the Dragon as well, somewhere to the east.

ChanderNagor will be the end of this. The earth speaks it to me even as I sit upon these low hills.

Grimacing, he got to his feet and moved further into the fields. Quail took flight around him in the tall grass, and a winter hare watched from a clump of brown wheat as he moved over a stone wall and continued to follow the army.

By mid-day the force had taken to the hills south of the road, their course concealed as they made their way further east. Farmsteads here were plentiful, but all were abandoned, the war having drawn the peasants into the city like a body drawing warmth away from fingers and toward more vital organs when frostbite sets in.

Relan released the force and kept on toward ChanderNagor. The city was ancient, and so it had many civilized roots – like those of a giant tree – that crept from its main center and spread out into the land around it.

Small communities appeared, some destroyed and others like empty tombs, snow covering them all in a fine white powder.

Wars are not meant to be fought in the snow. This entire campaign was spurred on by the unnatural.

It was dusk when he first saw the fires burning low and plentiful in the fields south of the city's mighty walls. Those high defensive works were forty feet in the lull and another twenty atop that at each tower. Engines of war were in place upon the battlements, massive trebuchets, catapults, and ballistae stood out in the fading daylight, and yet only a spare few warriors with flag-tipped lances walked among the hulking machines.

Jumping up on a stone in the lee of field, Relan extended his sight and turned his focus to the sieging army outside the walls.

Impossible.

Amid the fires men walked with banners emblazoned with the symbols of Human nobility. Horse and knight were among those encamped, and beyond them the gates of the city stood open.

He searched the field until a small rise in the open plain shown with the lamps and banners of the King of Aflyr. The grand tent was set out with only a modicum of defensive pickets and men marched about in surcoats instead of armor.

The madness that befell Lystbrook has taken hold here as well, for only a fool would defend his nation outside walls designed to withstand even a great tide of Delvers and Ruks.

Looking to the southeast, another set of fires dotted the fields there, and a dark shadow of earth had fallen over the land like a black plague.

The Delver host, and the King means to meet them in the open field.

Jumping down, Relan withdrew to the western road and slipped across the way as darkness fell. It wasn't hard to pick up the Mahe Army's tracks as they wound up into the hills and forest, clearly planning to slip east and then into the middle-ranges between the two armies.

When he entered the trees, the scent of the Wyrm permeated his senses. He made his way through the tangles and bows until the army's pickets held him at bay.

You are close, great beast, but I'll wait here. There is no use wasting precious energy slipping inside the camp when dawn will find the army on the march once more.

Settling into the hollow of a tree, he pulled his cloaks about him and closed his eyes as the fabric took on the aspect of the tree's bark. Beyond his position, no fires burned, but men moved about and horses tramped in the snow, and he listened cautiously until sleep came to him in fitful cascades.

CHAPTER NINE

IGRAYN

There is a moment when everything you believe in must come into focus, be tested, and then one way or the other you will be irrevocably changed.

For me, that day is today, my path having finally led to the doorstep of the man I am to marry, with both a Dragon at my back, and a dark enigma professing to be my love at my side.

Now the Ghost Moon hangs high, its bloody sister coming from the north like a savage, and the winds of war blowing fetid from the plain beyond this line of sheltering trees. I must take up my place as defender of Aflyr, accept my burden, and be done with dreams of a foolish girl. Tomorrow my life will be changed forever, and that is something I can no longer avoid.

"There is another army among these hills," the Dragon rumbled.

The small company sat amid the sheltering trees, the fires outside ChanderNagor glowing like stars in the fields far beneath the slope.

"Three armies?" Ash asked.

"It will be the force from Nehru, but I don't know why they haven't gone to join the King," Tavalori answered.

"Because whoever leads them is no fool," the Dragon replied.

Igrayn stood in the shadows, her furs pulled around her near-naked form and hair frosted with white. She watched the fires a moment longer before letting her eyes trail to the trees.

Who leads that force now? Braxus? Sire FreeAxe? Some Cursed Knight of Mahe? And what of Erik? Where will he have fled to now?

"What are you thinking?" Ash asked.

She looked down at the Eldaryn, his warmth melting the snow from the tips of her boots.

"I was wondering if I should deliver myself to the King or if I could instead make my way to the forest camp and stay with the Company of the Coast until I'm forced to leave," she replied.

He smiled, the light of the Ghost Moon making his cheeks shine. "Something tells me you should find the rest of the Company, even if we don't know exactly who that is."

She nodded, "Indeed, but I'll go alone. There is no use in bringing the Dragon to the camp, and I'll need you to watch of him."

Tavalori stepped up, clutching his bow, but she stayed him with a hand. "I must do this, alone, and if I don't return, both of you must see the Dragon to the field because whatever was summoned in the South is still out there."

The Dragon squinted an orange eye at her, but did not protest and Tavalori turned and stalked back to the trees he'd been keeping watch from.

"Watch him as well," she whispered.

Ash nodded and she turned to go, her black boots crunching snow as she walked along the ridgeline to the dark camp amid the trees.

She moved forward, the guards she'd acquired at the pickets falling back as Erik walked from his tent. In the dim light, his face was pale, and his eyes grew wide when he approached her.

"How?" he asked.

"It is a long story," she replied.

He reached out, but withdrew his hand, blinking and turning to Telluria. Beside him Wizard appeared between two knights, the sea rolling in with her.

"You said…" he began before his words were drowned by hers.

"I said Igrayn was dead, yes, but because I needed to know what true purpose you served in Aflyr," Telluria stated.

Igrayn stared at the Wizard, her friend, and found her lips tightening.

You left me in the clutches of the Wyrm and then fled north to fill Erik's ears with news of my death! What game do you play?

"If you hadn't saved my life from the Fey…" Erik hissed.

"Fey?" Igrayn asked.

Erik turned back to her, eyes dark and hand flexing on the hilt of *Fury*. "Yes, the creature attempted to take me to the Second World, but Telluria sent it back instead."

So it was you who took on the challenge, Telluria, and now I see more clearly why you were forced to leave me.

"Then the world is in a better place for her interference, no matter what lies she may have told either of us in the process," Igrayn said.

Erik turned back and shook his head, the moon's full light braking through a thin cloud to bathe her in silver light. His breath caught in his throat, and Telluria spoke up.

"I see the Dragon has accepted you as his bride," the Wizard said.

"Bride?" Erik croaked.

Igrayn nodded, "Yes. It's why the Fey came for you. Telluria brought me to the Dragon so that I might charm it into siding against the enemy."

Men shifted in their armor, eyes taking her in. The distance from the Dragon was finally allowing cold to prick her skin, and she drew the furs closer around her chest.

"Then you've…" Erik broke off the rest of his thought.

"It is a Dragon, Erik, don't let your imagination get the better of you. A "bride" is simply a partner and guide in this world until he returns to his slumber," Telluria said.

He let out a long breath, but then pointed, "But the clothing, or lack thereof."

"It was the Dragon's wish his bride be dressed so, and that she carry the gifts he provided," Igrayn answered, letting the fur fall aside so that she could show all those gathered the blade at her naked hip.

"And where is this Dragon?" Erik asked.

"In the trees further east, along with Ash and Tavalori."

At the mention of Tavalori, Erik's face twisted into a frown. "Then he has done you no favors. You are shivering," he said.

Igrayn replaced the blade and pulled the furs closer, but the shaking continued. "I am too far from his fire."

"Bring the princess some clothing," Erik commanded.

Knights started to move, but she stopped them, "No! I must be his until the battle is finished. We can't lose him. I will return to him and the others and bring them back the camp."

Erik nodded, "Very well, but stay within the trees. We can't afford to let the enemy know we are here."

"And what of the King, does he know you are here?" she asked.

"No, and we will keep it that way until the battle begins. Better to lay in wait and use surprise where we can."

"Even if it hinders the King's plans?"

Erik continued to frown, "The King has taken the field, fled his walls, and jeopardizes all of ChanderNagor. I will not trust him to know my presence, not with his complete lack of strategy fully in play for all to see."

Well played, and I must agree it is fruitless to waist your advantage when the battle is already laid out for all to see.

"Very well. I will return within the hour, and then I will be at your disposal," she said.

Her guards returned with her to the pickets, and by the time she slipped back onto the ridge her chills had gone, the power and protection of the Wyrm blanketing her.

CHAPTER TEN

ERIK

She's returned, perhaps not from the dead as I was led to believe, but returned nonetheless. Now my actions weigh more heavily than before. As I looked at her last night I was nearly overcome with a need to possess her, a desire like nothing I've ever felt.

Perhaps that is the will of the Wyrm, the trick it is playing dressing her in such a fashion and parading her about in front of a man who could die on the morrow, and would give their eye teeth for one last night with a woman, or at least with the right woman.

If so, it has worked on me to perfection, and now I stand on the threshold of war and can think of nothing but tawdry nights and spent passions. That is surely a fine recipe for defeat, for death, and yet I can think of no better reason to survive to see another day. Instead of distraction I must turn this into focus, and walk the razors edge to a new destiny.

Leading SmokeShadow up to the edge of the tree line, Erik looked out at the half-mile of farmlands known as the Brass Fields. Trodden winter-wheat tangled in a gold and white carpet between the pavilions of King NyWinter and the walls of ancient ChanderNagor.

His breath misted in the morning air as the sun still hung low and red on the eastern horizon. Beside him the rest of his war council took positions, their eyes taking in what the scouts had reported during their rounds in the false dawn.

King NyWinter had a powerful host of bannered and armored heavy cavalry at his center, just beyond bowshot from his own walls. He had also accumulated an impressive collection of four thousand foot who defended the right and left flanks of his knights. Crossbowman held positions along the southern gate of the city, and the king's personal pavilion and banners lay well defended at the colorful center of his many pickets and columns of foot soldiers in reserve.

Across a no-mans-land of crisp white snow sprawled the Delver horde, their dark banners and smoking fire-lines showing their determination to wage a war against the Knights of ChanderNagor, no matter the cost in lives.

Even with his numbers at near ten thousand, the Jai-Ruk commander has to understand the terrible toll those knights will cause once they split his army in twain with a charge.

"The old king may not have needed us after all," Sire FreeAxe commented gruffly at Erik's left side.

For some reason I don't feel victory here, but from the way the battlefield is currently laid out, there is little cause to argue with those words.

"Sire FreeAxe, can you take your Kin east along the trees until you come to the coast road? There you can stop any Delver retreat as you wait for my signal to attack," Erik instructed.

FreeAxe smiled and beat his gauntleted fist against his armored chest before leaving the hill with is female sub-commanders in tow.

Erik's eyes still watched the display on the field as the morning sun painted the entire scene in shades of blood. Somewhere inside him his ancestors warned that this would be a day of slaughter, and the itching feeling that produced in his conscience stayed his hand, at least until he could deduce where the hidden pitfalls lay.

"Braxus, Malcolm, I want both of you to return to your men and ready them along the western slopes of the forest. When we attack, you will be responsible for sweeping into the Delver's left flank should they manage to overwhelm the king's footmen," Erik continued.

The two men nodded, the Malcolm motioning for Telurria to follow him back to his men. After a moment of pause, she turned and went with his Captains.

Good, she'll be out of my way but close if need be, and with her Malcolm should see another sunrise.

Behind him some five hundred foot, the remainder of his Cursed Lancer Company and the Inlander reserves, waited in the thick forest. Beside him Captain Bloodstar and the now enchanted "Dragon Princess" still stood, waiting for their personal orders.

"Captain, I want you to bring up my standard bearer. Our forces will need to see that banner when we call for the attack."

Bloodstar bowed and backed away before summoning one of her lieutenants, sending word for the lancers to mount up and come forward.

Erik continued to study the arrayed Delvers on the field.

The deployment makes no sense. It's as if they are afflicted with the same insanity as the King.

As the forces waited, a rider burst from the main gate of the city, his cloak flying and his hand whipping the reins back and forth over the horse's shoulders. Behind him, deep within the city, smoke rose like a stain of ink against the morning sky.

Erik licked his lips against the cold; waving away a word from Igrayn as he watched the rider. The man flew like the wind, while the morning bells of the city's gardens filled the crisp air with calls for the grace of the God of Light.

When the rider made the tents of the Knights of ChanderNagor and the King, he dismounted and ran about the roused nobility waving his arms wildly and pointing back to the city. Above the gate, remaining guards dashed about like a nest of disturbed ants, but the gates remained open exacerbating the current vulnerability of the city.

"Sir?" Captain Bloodstar questioned as she came back up and stood at his side.

Erik held up his hand, and the Captain stood down.

Knights in the reserves, true high nobles all, were now summoning steeds, and King NyWinter's pavilion was stirring. The king's east and west flanks were up as well, the sub-commanders and lieutenants sending messengers all over the lines looking for answers.

"Your Grace!" announced Erik's herald, the youth coming forward with the azure banner of Mahe in his hands, the smiling mermaid looking very pleased with her beauty in the morning light. Erik didn't turn, but nodded to the young man before he raised his right hand to ready the standard bearer for action.

"When I release my hand, you will run forward down the slope and plant the standard in the clearing," Erik said, and the young man bowed.

Further down on the Brass Fields, the knights were now mounted and riding full tilt back to the open gates of the city without banner or fanfare. From Erik's viewpoint on the hill, he made out King NyWinter half-adorned with shining plate and calling out around his pavilion for order. The King's words rang into nothingness as his vaunted heavy cavalry were already on the thundering path back to his capital city.

Amid the confusion the drummers of the Delver horde let loose a thunderous cacophony that set the King's army turning in confusion. With the distraction from the city, the Delver host had crept forward, lines of Ruk archers sprinting half the distance of the field to gain range. In howling rush the Delver vanguard now advanced, a hail of black-shafted arrows from the archers releasing death into the right and left of the king's force.

Men screamed, and trumpets sounded as the king's foot formed up against the rush of the Delvers. In places the units couldn't set themselves fast enough, their lines breaking and causing lanes for the Delver runners to slip through.

Erik heard the boom of the gates' closure even before he saw the knights in the retreating vanguard halt before them. Horses reeled and men cursed. The once well-guarded gatehouse had become a ghost tower, the scrambling guards replaced by empty turrets and vacant murder holes.

Erik kept his hand raised as a black form rose on the upper gate with a huge pot of pitch in its grotesque and powerful arms. It was fifteen feet tall, with legs of a beast and a topknot of hair above its manly face. With a great scream, it threw the smoking fluid down on the knights circling below. Horses screamed and men burned as the dark mass fell among them. The beast leapt after the spray, jumping down from the seventy foot wall like a man taking a stair two steps at a time.

Chain demon!

Behind Erik, Captain Bloodstar strangled a warning, but Erik kept his hand raised.

I've seen these creatures before, in the Planar Archipelago. Now I know the true purpose of the Dragon.

"Igrayn, you should find your Wyrm. The two of you will need to protect one another in this coming battle," Erik spoke without emotion.

His eyes studied the King's crumbling left, then the demon among the knights at the ChanderNagor gate, and the now oncoming Jai-Ruk middle charging King NyWinter's pavilion in full stride.

"I would stay with you," Igrayn replied.

Turning, Erik reached out and grabbed her by a black leather bracer. She turned, her eyes going from his to the battle and then back again. Beside them Bloodstar cleared her throat, but Erik held both Igrayn and his own arm in check.

"Why? That thing must be dealt with!" he asked.

"I would ask you the same question. You still hold your force, when a counter now into the Delver flank would break their assault," she answered.

"I have my reasons," he said.

"And I mine."

They stared at one another, Bloodstar now shifting her weight from one foot to another. Erik bit his lip, the blood inside him pumping so fast he could hear it in his ears.

"Sir!" Bloodstar prompted, taking a step up to him.

Erik broke eye contact with Igrayn. As he released her arm, the heat and smell of the sea created a mist of snow in the air.

"Igrayn, you will be with me, as will your Wyrm. The new problem at the gate will need to be dealt with," Erik said as he looked back to Bloodstar.

Bloodstar was flushed at the cheeks, her eyes darting to the battle and back to Erik until she could hold her tongue no longer, "Commander, the king's defense, it is in jeopardy!"

Erik looked up the tree line to the slopes where Braxus and Malcolm waited with his two thousand battle-hardened troops. Letting out a curse he spun back to the battle and took in the carnage.

Bloodstar was right; King NyWinter was in desperate peril as the lethal Jai-Ruk reavers cut down both his honor guard and the city watch defensive platoons with only minimal resistance. At the gate, the knights had either died at the hands of the demon or been sent riding randomly into the waiting walls of Delver runners who had bypassed the army's right flank defense in the initial assault.

Behind the King the pressed infantry that comprised the left flank had all but collapsed in confusion, offering only random pockets of resistance as a few charmed lieutenants somehow rallying their men in a final stand. The King's right was in better condition, its men regulars from the standing army, and their commanders more seasoned, but numbers would tell within the hour if no further help came to them. There would be no escape routes to the gate or the sea, the Jai-Ruk commanders having already cut off all avenues of escape.

"Erik?" Igrayn questioned as well, but he said nothing as he watched the slaughter unfold below him.

Bloodstar and the standard bearer exchanged glances. Igrayn placed a hand on Erik's shoulder. Her eyes were now wet with tears as she watched the valiant defense of the men of ChanderNagor, their last banners tattered and bloodied as more and more men fell to Delver cleaver, scimitar, and axe.

"Don't do this..." Igrayn whispered.

Erik watched, eyes unblinking as each knight was pulled under in a sea of black and red, and every noble pavilion ground down in the onslaught of steel-toed boots. Beyond the king's rise, the Chain Demon had brought forth a mighty ball and chain the length again the size of a full grown man. It championed death with each sweeping blow, felling Delver and Human alike as it moved inexorably toward the king and his remaining banners.

Something drives this. Something moves the battle like a puppet-master.

Turning from the destruction, he let his gaze fall over the near-abandoned Delver camp. Smoking firepits, tattered tents, and scavenged supply lay about in some chaotic fashion, but amid the darkness a woman stood.

There you are!

She was tall, pale-skinned with hair like midnight to match the strips of cloth tightly drawn over her near-naked body. Beside her a man stood, his skin bronze and head bald, with a spear in one hand and a curved blade at his hip.

"Priestess," he hissed.

"What?" Igrayn and Bloodstar asked in unison.

"Bloodstar, look there," Erik pointed.

Bloodstar was at his shoulder in an instant. Erik's finger cast down to the Delver camp to help the Captain see what he had seen.

"Who is she?" Bloodstar asked.

"When I give the order to attack, and I will give that order, you will take Todmann down to the camp and find an answer to that question," Erik answered.

Bloodstar nodded before turning on her heel and returning to her lancer company deeper in the brown and white forest.

Only Erik, Igrayn, and the standard bearer remained to watch the final stand of King NyWinter and his valiant men-at-arms. The King's brilliant armor was still virginal and bright in the shining light of full morning when the first of the Jai-Ruks made it to him. A runed blade shown in his hand, but the Ruk deflected a feeble strike, and repaid the attack with a blow that removed the monarch's arm at the elbow. Erik could see the open mouth of the King's scream, but the sound was lost to the battle. The massive Ruk blasted the King from his feet with another stroke of his two-handed cleaver, the weapon's upward-pointing tip piercing the king's breastplate and spraying royal blood into the cold morning air.

Erik said a quiet prayer for the men who had given their lives to defend such a useless man.

A man of wealth and leisure is a fool to strap on armor and pretend at soldiering.

With the fall of their liege, the King's position was quickly and completely lost in a wave of black and red Ruks. Looking at last to the standard bearer, Erik locked eyes with the boy who stared at him like he had seen a lord of the abyss in the flesh.

Without a word, Erik dropped his arm and the boy swallowed once before sprinting forward with the banner flapping in the air above him.

"Why?" Igrayn whispered from beside him.

"If you have to ask, you're not the woman who was worth the lives I just spent," Erik replied.

Before she could respond, trumpeters of the Army of Mahe called into the morning air, a flood of armed and armored men rushing after the call onto the Brass Fields.

CHAPTER ELEVEN

RELAN

*W*ar *is not the way of the Druid. Our work is sometimes subtle, sometimes furious, but is always within the confines of the natural order. Conflict such as this is far beyond the realm that we rule over, and yet I am here amid the death and destruction that is the very antithesis of the life I would chose to live.*

Now, I feel the presence of another god, or perhaps several, their will playing out on all those willing to lay down their lives for a cause not truly theirs.

Delvers swarmed through the fields, and Relan walked among them, his cloaks pulled close and his staff raised. The army passed around him, like water around a stone, and his lips whispered the words of the wood, of stone, and of grass.

He moved past the lines, through the muck of churned mud and wheat until the Delver camp stretched before him. The din of war was like thunder behind him, but he moved on, the stink of the goddess snaked its way into his nose and putt a chill in his bones.

Across the wasteland lay a panoply of skin tents, the remnants of the Delver camp. His bare feet marched forward until the call of trumpets gave him pause. Turning, he watched a charge of Human lancers from the trees to the south, a mass of foot soldiers following the rush.

Only now do you join the battle? Late is the hour, and some other game is played here.

The smell of earth, unfettered by corruption rolled over him, and he looked back to the Delver camp. From the east another army surged, this one a huge collection of Kin. Sires, towering and hawk-faced lumbered through a host of armor-plated females as the force rushed the reserves and rear flank of the enemy of mankind.

A powerful host indeed, and the Sires have brought forth the full fury of their element for battle, their transformation into Lizard-Kin complete.

As awesome as the sight was, he had more pressing matters. Moving forward, he walked directly into the path of the new army, staff held before him as the ground trembled with the might of their rush. The Kin swept north, into the enemy supply and then crushed the Delver reserves, hedging close to the city walls to the north. The bulk of the abandoned camp was left unspoiled, and it was there the stink of the goddess was most profound.

He kept on, and as he moved through the tents, the sound of hooves turned his attention away from his final goal. A dozen lancers, men with blue tabards and armor of burnished bronze charged into the camp. At their head, a female knight and a stout man in amber robes and chain rode, the man's hands on the reins of his steed and holding a jade talisman aloft that glowed with white fire.

Another priest! The gods play here in more ways than I expected...

The force outpaced him, and he began to jog, the mix of magic and the elements clouding his senses until a wisp of foreign power brought his eyes to the rear of the charging force. There, amid the knights was a man in forest brown, a bow across his saddle and the guise of humanity wrapping something all-together different.

Tavalori!

Relan broke into a full run, but the company was charging now, and from further ahead a wave of dark magic struck like a quake. He lost his footing when the force hit him, his staff turning to fire as the birds resisted the spell. Around him, the air was filled with ash, smoke, and dirt that swirled in the shapes of skulls and groping hands.

"Oak Father, bless me with your strength," he whispered.

The trio of firebirds flared and his feet pushed off until he stood once more. A rider-less horse bolted past him, eyes wild and mouth trailing black froth. The ring of steel broke clear in the morning air, and he struggled forward as nausea faded from his stomach.

Amid the ruin of tents laid flat by the magic blast, corpses lay with arms and legs twisted like dolls tossed aside by a careless child. He stopped, bent down to the face of a man, the corpse's eyes wide and black as polished onyx as he stared at the sky.

What power is this? What work has been done to claim such venomous strength?

He waved a hand and closed the man's eyes, a scream breaking over the battlefield. Rising again, he saw figures now amid the settling swirls of corruption from the initial blast.

The woman was there, her hands black and swirling with sickly yellow runes, her teeth bared as the amber priest held his jade talisman aloft before her. The man had a spiked mace in his left hand and swung it, the priestess catching it in one hand even as the weapon's spikes pierced her flesh.

She screamed and the ground shook, her blood dripping down the weapon's haft like a dozen serpents until the rivulets sank into the man's hand and wormed their way beneath the skin. He fell back a step, calling on the power of his deity with a dry, cracked voice, even as the light of his talisman sparked and then dimmed.

Relan turned from the central conflict, eyes searching the circle. A single knight still stood, blade in hand as she clashed with a tan giant of a man who wielded a spear tipped with obsidian along one side of the point.

Where is Tavalori?

The bowman was not among those near him, and he moved off, the amber priest's voice rising as he drew on some other favor of his god. Three bodies lay in a tangle, and he pushed the one atop with his staff for a clearer view of those beneath. The body was half-moved when an arm shot out and grabbed the staff.

Relan fell back, but the grip of the man was strong and held the staff in place as the bodies began to untangle. They were all knights, but now black bile dripped from their lips and those same onyx eyes stared lifeless from blue-veined faces.

Pressing the staff down instead of resisting, Relan brought forth words to his patron.

"From the earth's wellspring
I ask for fire from the deep
Bring forth your heat
And cleanse this corruption from your body"

Flame, blue as the evening sky, burst from the tip of the *Phoenix Staff* and blasted a hole through armor and flesh alike. One corrupted knight fell back, flame trailing from his open mouth, and Relan turned the fire on the other two.

Flesh cooked, yet they drew blades, and rose from the ash of the field. He turned his grip, wielding the staff as a flaming spear, and cut the head from one of the attackers as the second raised his sword to strike.

An arrow, yew shafted and owl fletched struck the knight through the forehead, the undead thing's strike fell wide. Relan turned his staff again and struck the wounded creature down, flame slicing metal and bone from neck to stomach.

From his right, Tavalori rose from the camp ruin, bow in hand and another arrow ready.

Thank the Oak Father!

Another scream tore from the amber priest, and Relan looked away from Tavalori as the man fell back, his talisman tumbling from racked fingers and his body convulsing with bone snapping twitches. The priestess stood over him, blood trailing from a wicked smile upon her lips.

An arrow, the hiss cutting the field, struck the priestess in the throat and knocked her back a step.

"Tavalori, no!" Relan yelled.

The priestess blinked, the black and yellow runes from her hands slithering up her arms and coalescing at her neck. There was a snap, and the arrow fell free, one half behind and one before.

What demons have you lain with to achieve such power?

Raising his staff, Relan called again to the Oak Father.

"Gail of the north,
Hurricane of the south,
Bring me your strength
Empower me with your force"

Even before the words had finished, the priestess raised her hands and black energy rose in a perfect circle around her in a thirty foot ring. Tavalori, now standing and readying another arrow was caught in the circle and a scream tore through him as he dropped the bow and fell to his knees.

Relan turned the *Phoenix Staff* and aimed the firebirds at the priestess, a shockwave of air launching from it like the strike of a Titan's maul. She was blasted from her circle, blood erupting from her mouth and bones shattering on impact.

Beyond the ring, the spearman fell back from his combat with the knight, his long strides taking him to his fallen mistress, but Relan lowered his staff and moved around the still smoldering darkness of the enchanted circle until he was within five feet of Tavalori.

The young man wept, his tears black, and his hands palm up and stained yellow on his thighs.

"Tavalori, I am your father's servant, and I have come to deliver you home," Relan said.

The sobs slowly turned to laughter, the stink of the goddess so strong it brought bile to Relan's throat.

Tavalori turned, eyes shining black in the sun even as the circle stole the light of day like a thief.

"Do you know the power?" he asked.

Relan, knuckles white on the *Phoenix Staff*, shook his head, "No."

"All would have been denied me, stolen from me, as I wasted a life in the woods," Tavalori said.

Relan shook his head, "A life in the service of nature is not a life wasted."

Tavalori laughed again, "So you would have me believe, but I have seen the world now, came close to tasting its fruits, and now my eyes are fully open to what I can have."

"These promises, this power, it is a veil that masks the suffering that will come with it," Relan replied.

"Suffering? Suffering?!" Tavalori repeated. "What do you know of suffering until you watch the years pass without a single companion? What pain have you felt when the one beauty you have ever known is denied you again and again by the tricks of little gods and the fickle nature of a woman?"

"This is not you. It is your mother speaking," Relan said.

"My mother would keep me at her side, and not hide me away in a shack!" Tavalori raged. "She would see me a king, with a bride to match my lineage at my side. Would you deny that?"

Relan shook his head, "No."

Tavalori laughed as he rose to his feet. "Then I will take her now, and make all this land my own in the name of my mother."

"Then I am sorry," Relan whispered.

"Why?" Tavalori asked.

The *Phoenix Staff* blazed again, another blast of air stuck Tavalori at point blank range, his body shattering on impact. He was thrown twenty feet, beyond the now still corpse of the amber priest and into the ash piles at the feet of the spearman.

Standing, Relan sighed and took a step toward the fallen godling before the ground trembled. He righted himself, but the darkness of the circle grew. He saw the spearman lift two bodies in his arms, place one on either shoulder as the ash swirled and the amber priest's body broke open and darkness exploded into the air.

A hand grabbed him, and he turned with staff ablaze at the attack. The female knight, her face ashen and trailing blood, was pulling him away.

"Run!" the woman screamed.

Relan looked back, the spearman gone and the darkness coalescing into a giant that trailed chains with links half the size of a man's forearm.

It is done, and my mission failed, but I fear the journey here is not at an end, not without the body that must be returned to my master.

Turning, Relan followed the fleeing knight through the broken camp, a bellow of anger and pain rising into the sky behind him.

CHAPTER TWELVE

ERIK

*A*nd *so either comes my doom or my salvation. Only time will tell which.*

"Where is Tavalori?" Erik asked.

"He went with Bloodstar," Ash answered.

Erik looked at the trees, a small company of riders barely visible at the verge.

You shadow the princess all these weeks, and now during the final battle you would abandon her?

Trumpets blew again, and he righted SmokeShadow, then placed his boots into his mounts sides. The horse leapt forward, Igrayn and the rest of the lancers following as the army moved from the cover of the trees.

The Cursed Legion broke fast, moving down-slope into the fields and charging a confused line of outlying Delvers at the far side of the fallen king's left flank. The Delver force, spurred on by the whips of the Ruks, had overextended to reach the King's pavilion, and the lancers blasted through their line in a killing wave, Erik's charge unbroken as he sped into the heart of the enemy middle.

Each lance was tipped with three feet of sharpened steel that ended in a flower-petal barb. The weapons sliced through the Delver defense as Ruks blew horns and screamed orders in black speech that went unheard in the rout.

Erik loosened his grip on his lance and shook his shoulder as he approached a dark line of targets. Speed would become a disadvantage if you held your weapon too tight and it became lodged in an opponent.

Would my warmasters be proud that I learned their lessons well enough that I did not become one of those young cavaliers who broke or dislocated their shoulders on charges like this?

Igrayn shouted something beside him, but her words were lost in the din of thundering hooves. He tipped his lance low and impacted the chest of a Jai-Ruk, the warrior unable to dodge the strike due to his proximity to his milling companions. Releasing his grip on the lance, Erik urged SmokeShadow up and over the falling enemy and into the second row of Delvers behind.

All along the line, the five hundred light lancers struck into the very heart of the enemy, their charge crippling the loosely fabricated defense and sending hardened Jai-Ruk warriors away from their tight rows.

The air rang with the sound of blades leaving sheaths, the cavalry going to swords in the confines of close combat. Men cursed, and their trained horses wheeled and kicked at the enemy, protecting their riders from the close-in hacks of Delver cleavers and scimitars.

Fury sang against the helmet of a Delver as Erik spun about looking at the sea of black around him. The Jai-Ruk middle still comprised near three thousand veteran troops, and although his charge was a success, the tide would again turn in favor of the Ruks if ground support didn't reach his cavalry soon.

"I still want to know!" Igrayn screamed beside him, her ancient blade blocking an enemy scimitar and then riposting with a blinding strike across the enemy's eyes.

Erik repressed a smile before turning an enemy axe from its path. Cursing, he put his boots into the hindquarters of SmokeShadow, his heels sending the horse's hooves up and out, taking an enemy squarely in the chest. The horse's strike sent the unfortunate soul tumbling back into three of his charging compatriots.

"If we survive this, then you can hate me!" Erik called back. With a quick cleave, he took a Jai-Ruk in the back, splitting the warrior's neck plate and spewing blood five feet up into the air.

Around the pair a dozen more lancers rallied in defense. Without a line, each sought a holding position in the churning sea of enemy bodies.

"It would be my please!" Igrayn called back. The princess again found a vulnerable spot in the armor of an oncoming Delver, spilling dark blood over the snow and mud beneath her horse.

Erik's eyes found the fallen king's pavilion knoll in the distance and he called to his command. "Lieutenant Gariaus, call the advance to my banner, I'm taking that hill!"

Putting his heels into SmokeShadow's flanks, he moved north into the oncoming Delver resistance.

The blood-splattered Gariaus swung his longsword a final time before reaching to his saddle and pulling up an ivory horn. With a clarion call, the trumpeter signaled the order up and down the field, the sub-commanders spurring their steeds toward their duke. Erik used *Fury* as a marker, the blade glowing above the path he cut north to the fallen king's small lookout knoll.

Behind Erik, his standard waved like a ship on a storm-tossed sea, the remaining lancers of his personal command struggling behind him, their blades hacking up and down in the light of the new dawn.

The hill was rising beneath him as SmokeShadow reared up. Erik cursed as he was pulled from the saddle by strong hands. Swinging to his left with *Fury*, he cut the hand from one of the Jai-Ruks who held SmokeShadow, but then he fell backward and down, his Fey breastplate impacting the muddy earth. A steel-toed boot caught his head and set his helmet spinning off. He managed to raise his left arm as a scimitar raked the armored bracer and sent sharp pain across his forearm.

Blood was everywhere. He tried to get *Fury* up when a shadow fell over the sun. Ruks, once ready to end his life, looked up and the smell of brimstone washed away the stink of earth. A roar shook the ground, and flame bathed the field. The Dragon had come.

Erik took advantage of the distraction and slashed madly with *Fury*. Quickly the Ruk legs backed away from his vision, replaced by the hooves of more of his loyal lance company as they swiftly surrounding him. Curses in black speech rained around the field while he got to his feet. Yet his sudden salvation was cut short when a huge Ruk chieftain blasted Lieutenant Gariaus from his saddle and rallied the dark troops back into the press.

"No lying down now!" Igrayn called, spurring her horse forward and swinging at the new adversary.

Erik was about to warn the brash princess, but his words hadn't even left his mouth before the Jai-Ruk leader rolled to his knees and cut the front legs from Igrayn's horse with a single swing of his two-handed cleaver.

The princess flew forward from her saddle, Ash going after her, and Erik rushed toward the conflict with his blade outstretched. The Jai-Ruk turned to meet his charge, their weapons clashing as they engaged in single combat.

The Jai-Ruk was massive, his body covered in rhino armor, fur, and trophies of war, the newest being the head of King NyWinter. The monarch's dead eyes stared out into the oblivion he now faced.

Erik flicked *Fury* around and under the war cleaver, the length of the blade drawing a bloody wound up the chief's right arm, but the Ruk didn't notice. Swinging down with incredible strength, the chief impacted *Fury* and sent sparks into the cold mud. Erik adjusted his grip to a two-handed hold and backed away, his arms screaming after having taken such a blow.

The Jai-Ruk wasn't done, and somehow adjusted his own powerful swing enough to whip his blade back up and down in a kind of windmill strike that sent Erik reeling yet again. Turning away a moment, Erik ducked right and then brought *Fury* back across his body, making another accurate strike across the chief's armored thighs. *Fury's* magic cut the rhino hide plates and spilled blood out, yet again the Jai-Ruk gave no reaction.

The earth empowers him, and he feels nothing.

Erik was vulnerable for a split second after the attack and the chief didn't miss any opportunity. Using one of his studded gauntlets, the chief struck Erik with a powerful backhand that lifted him from his feet and sent him sprawling onto the field of bodies now covering the area.

Erik shook away stars as blood washed down his cheek, the image of the oncoming Jai-Ruk flooding him with much needed adrenaline. He calmed his mind enough to let the chief come on, the warrior moving close in his attempt for a full downward swing of his cleaver.

Erik used the proximity to kick up and out with his own boot against the Jai-Ruk's knee, using all the strength his prone body could muster.

Bones cracked and gave, the impact throwing the chief's blow to the side so that Erik rolled away and scrambled across the bloodied corpses as he got to his feet. Even limping, the chief was fast, his shattered knee only slowing him enough that he had to use his two-handed weapon in one great black fist.

Erik turned again, righting his perception, *Fury* coming up and again blocking away a dooming strike by the chief. From the corner of his vision, he saw a flash of metal before the chief grunted and stumbled forward. Erik capitalized on the moment's loss of concentration and lunged at his enemy, his blade taking the Jai-Ruk full into his armored throat. Forcing *Fury* through the chief's neck, he watched another smaller blade emerge from the Ruk's chest spilling dark fluid down the front of the armor.

Horns blared around him then, and Erik saw the light in the Jai-Ruk's eyes fade and go dark. Horse's hooves and the cheering of men erupted from the field, the men of the foot flowing among both the dead and living along the knoll. Braxus had arrived and his men relieved the hard-pressed remnants of the Mahe Lancers.

Erik pulled *Fury* from the chief's neck and kicked the body sideways, his vision falling on the disheveled and bloodied form of Igrayn, her equally bloody blade held before her with two hands. Beside her, Ash stood bleeding and whispering prayers to Bandylegs.

"He killed my horse..." she whispered.

Somewhere down the hill, thunder boomed and the earth shook, the Dragon landing on a huge stone as it blew fire into the face of the oncoming Chain Demon. Erik was about to call for a horse when Igrayn fell forward and he caught her with his free hand. He held her to his chest, the ragged sounds of her breathing drawing at his heart. It was only then that he noticed the ragged wound along her unarmored abdomen.

Adjusting his grip on *Fury*, he placed the blade between them and whispered the sword's name. From within the blade, a wave of magic flowed out between them, the healing power of the Planes dividing and knitting both their wounds, yet not powerful enough steal away the lingering pain.

He could feel time adjusting around them both, Igrayn's breathing steadying and her head coming away from his chest enough that she could catch his eyes.

"Will we ever stop saving each other?" she asked.

"I hope not," he replied.

He leaned close, the world shimmering around them, but then time slipped away and the battle returned. Braxus appeared, blood on his Ruk cleaver, and they pulled away from one another.

"Sorry to interrupt, but there is an issue with a demon to be dealt with," Braxus said drily.

"The Dragon has the Chain Demon, and it would be unwise to interfere," Erik replied.

"No, not that demon," Braxus pointed east, "*That* demon!"

Erik turned, another Chain Demon was moving from the Delver camp toward the heart of his force.

"If we don't stop that thing, we won't have an army left!" Braxus hissed.

Even now, the Kin Sires were moving, their force coming to intercept the thing, but it would exact a terrible toll on any who faced it, even the battle-hardened Sires.

Beside him, Igrayn faltered, a scream pulled from her throat. He looked down and she clutched her stomach, once again leaning on him for support.

"The Dragon, it is wounded, and without the Fey its power is failing," she whispered.

Then let us pray it has the strength to hold.

Erik helped Igrayn regain her footing and readjusted his grip on *Fury*, the blade glowing fiercely now that its magic having been called forth for the day.

"Signal the banners! We still have work that needs finishing," Erik ordered. Finding his footing, he marched with sword in hand off to the east. Behind him, the rest of his lances, along with Braxus and Igrayn, followed. Meanwhile the foot soldiers pursued the Delver retreat back toward the right flank.

Erik's fire kindled in his chest as he watched the towering demon pick up a horse and rider just ahead of his path. The thing's tree-like arms cast the pair away like a child's toy, its chains rattling down from its massive wrists as arms swung back toward the oncoming troop. It was the size of a giant, eighteen feet at the shoulder and covered in mottled black flesh that wrapped corded muscles and bulging veins.

It is more a beast than the one the Dragon fights. This one is fresh from the Abyssal walls and hot with torment.

Tightening his fingers on the hilt of *Fury*, he relaxed the muscles in his shoulders and whispered his former master's words 'be the air.'

To his left Braxus came on, his boots kicking up mud, with the diminutive Ash close at his heels fire rippling from his outstretched hands. The mercenary approached as the demon threw another screaming rider and steed thirty feet and then turned to face the newest onslaught. With a battle cry, Braxus lunged, and the demon reached down and caught the Ruk cleaver in his hand. The things black claws tightened on the weapon and a sound like shattering glass rent the air as it exploded into half a hundred shards.

Braxus rolled just as the demon stomped at him, the footfall shaking the earth as flying mud ringed the impact.

"By the Gods!" the hardened mercenary cursed, staggering back from the scene, his hand searching his leather battle harness for another weapon.

The demon came on, but from the far side of the impact the prayers of Ash could be heard casting some dire curse upon the demon as it passed him.

> "Steal thy strength and bind they toes,
> Make it so that nothing goes,
> Replace this thing's might with plight!
> Bandylegs, bless me with thy power."

The creature shifted as it came on, the bulk under its impenetrable skin shuddering against the magic of the diminutive priest at it was slowed to a halt.

Igrayn took her opportunity to rush in, her ancient blade stinging little streaks on the beast's right leg. The creature roared in pain, but hobbled forward as it continued no its slow advance toward Braxus. The mercenary had settled on a long dagger and wicked throwing axe, both of which he now unlimbered from his shoulder harness.

Erik, his movement fluid as he kept his heels up, swung *Fury* across the path of the demon, the magic-kissed blade scored a bloody hit on the thing's right arm.

The demon hissed as though bit by a wasp, the arm jumping up and away from Erik. Using the demon's withdrawal; he ducked under its legs and brought another blow home against the same thigh that Igrayn had just attacked.

Acidic blood shot over the battlefield, the fluid hissing and popping wherever it struck armor, flesh, and even earth. Igrayn backed away, her blade steaming with the corrosive blood, but she clutched the holy symbol at her throat and too whispered a prayer to her goddess.

Erik dodged around a whistling blow from the demon's left arm, the chain dangling along the forearm covered in the blood and flesh of dozen men less fortunate than he.

There was a flash of light and thunder boomed as blue lightning stuck the demon in the face. Telluria, robes muddied from combat, pulled her horse up short as Malcolm rode on, lance pointed directly at the demon's chest.

The beast blew a mighty, cursing roar from its ruined mouth into the midday sky, then swept an arm out that tore the mount from beneath Malcolm and sent him flying into the mud. Erik didn't hesitate, and again danced in to cut two more wicked strikes into the thing's pelvis and belly, the wounds gushing and expelling a vile smell into the entire area.

The demon raged and beat the air with its chains, the weight and fury of its blows tearing against the binding magic of Ash as it struggled to move. It swung its arms back and forth trying to clear Erik away from its lower half. The sheer madness of the attack caught Erik off guard, and when he dodged a bit too slowly the edge of the chain tore across his side, shredding armor and flesh as it sent his body spinning to the bloody ground.

Ash's voice again rose from somewhere in the piles of dead, his little voice laughing and spitting out another fell curse.

"Oil of the earth,
Know the place,
Mark of the trickster
Send the beast to its face!"

The demon turned toward Erik as he struggled to right himself, the world a shifting blur of movement and flashing lights. He could taste the tang of blood, and he spat crimson into one muddy hand.

Fifteen feet away the demon took a step, but the mud was now a mix of oil and its foot slid as its pelvis rent. In a screaming tumble, the beast went down, the earth shaking with its impact.

"Water heals and is the bringer of life,
Goddess bless me with thy power."

Igrayn whispered as she knelt and Erik blinked away the lights dancing in his vision. Erik felt the fire in his side calm and his vision focused on her face.

"Thank you." he croaked.

She helped him stand, and he watched as Braxus leapt from one piece of uncorrupted ground to another as he worked his way to the struggling demon.

Two fiery missiles, both the size of ballista bolts, struck the thing's thick skull, followed soon after by two more. Telluria's steed came close, her *Naming Staff* held aloft as she continued to focus on the beast. Malcolm joined them, the mercenary holding his side but still gripping his lance.

Braxus was nearly to the thing when it flung out a chain and smashed an island of dry earth he'd just vacated.

Screaming, the mercenary leapt the last few feet and plunged his dagger between two armored plates in the things hide. It responded with a howl, and rolled over, flinging Braxus into the oil with a splash.

Tellurai cast out her arm and a glowing wall appeared before Braxus as the demon cast its chain again with terrible force. The wall held, much to Braxus' obvious surprise, and Erik moved forward to reclaim *Fury* from the mud.

"For the Duke!" Malcolm screamed as he charged forward with this lance.

The mercenary's charge caught the demon in his ruined shoulder at a point left open and bleeding from one of Telluria's missiles. The demon howled again, whipping its chain backward and driving Malcolm away but unharmed.

Erik broke into a run, fire blasting away in his chest as his spark lit full and hot. He jumped over the slick ground, each step a practiced leap done a thousand times under the watchful eye of Shera, his former master. Tumbling once, and then thrusting up with his all the power in his legs; he jumped up and over the last span of oily ground with *Fury* held like a spear between both his clenched fists.

The blade found its mark, sinking like a needle through the pink flesh beneath the opening that Malcolm's attack had exposed. The demon roared and slumped forward, the arteries in its neck shorn by Erik's mystic steel. Not waiting for a counterattack, Erik ripped *Fury* free and then drove it back into the flesh, this time full to the hilt.

A soft whimper left the thing's throat, its outstretched arms folding in and its grotesque face falling to the muddied earth. More rancid and toxic blood oozed from the wounds and Erik's gauntlets and knee guards hissed at the contact.

With a curse, he withdrew *Fury* and then jumped from the thing's back. Spinning the steaming sword in his hand, he reversed the field, and then stuck the blade into a corpse, working to free his hands and legs from his armor.

Telluria dismounted and Igrayn followed the Wizard as they approached. Igrayn was as pale as a ghost, and she shivered in the cold that blew over the field. Looking back toward the battle, Erik saw pale wings disappearing in the sky to the west. Humans and Kin alike were celebrating a victory in pockets around the mass of dead.

"Braxus?" he asked, tossing a hissing gauntlet to the ground and flexing his fingers.

"Ash is with him, but he seems to be moving," Telluria answered.

"And your 'mate' seems to have done his job," Erik added toward Igrayn.

Igrayn nodded, and then dropped her sword, the weapon splattering in the mud at her feet.

"The battle is won..." Igrayn said slumping down and sitting in the mud. Her hair was wet and dangling down about the dirtied furs, and her body shook like a leaf in the autumn breeze.

Telluria removed her cloak and placed it over Igrayn's legs, as Erik sighed and called for a sub-commander. A young man in dented armor and muddied face appeared.

"Find Sire FreeAxe, tell him that the Delver Camp is secure. Have him get into the city, no matter what the remaining defenders have to say about it," he ordered.

Telluria leaned heavily on her staff and watched the field and city beyond, the hem of her robes stained with mud. Malcolm came to help support her, and Erik nodded, his eyes following theirs to the city.

The Battle of Brass Fields is over, and yet another war begins, this one for the succession to throne of Aflyr.

CHAPTER THIRTEEN

ERIK

With so many dead, I always question why I was one of those that survived. Am I somehow luckier than the rest, perhaps because of my goddess, or in the end does fate itself have a hand to play one me?

Perhaps that is why you remain, why you watch over me? Or, in the end, is it all up to the sages who will study this war and decide if I am the savior or the villain. One thing is clear, it was my decision to watch the king die, and that is a burden I must live with along with all the other trophies of conscience I've collected in my few years on this plane.

I sometimes wonder, if I grow to be an old man, how many lives will I have ground under my boot? If she here, Shera would counter with how many lives I've saved along the way. Whatever the case, I feel I'm not one to be friendly with, unless of course you enjoy seeing your life put in jeopardy.

Reports from the battle had been coming into the makeshift ducal pavilion located on the knoll King NyWinter once held for his command. Erik sat with a field surgeon from the Legion, the man stitching the various wounds still left bleeding on Erik's body after the final conflict with the demon.

From what he could tell, the city gates were a slaughterhouse, as were the noble villas inside the city that now smoldered in ruin.

The demon had done its gruesome work with blinding speed and incredible accuracy. The nobility in ChanderNagor, and – from other reports – the nobles all along the eastern coast as well, were all but extinct. Someone had been playing kingmaker in Aflyr, as the loss of the Mahe Noble Houses at Ixprys helped prove.

Malcolm had been sent to secure the King's palace and place loyal legion men in command of what remained of the city watch. Bells and criers sounded from every street in the city announcing and mourning the dead of the houses as well as their fallen King and even his son who had died at the gates. It was a tinderbox for riot, and without an immediate, firm hand the city would explode into a chaos of looting and burning that usually accompanied a changing of political power.

Erik's heralds were already inside the walls placing the banners of Mahe in the common squares. The announcement that the Duke of Mahe had won the day was being spread. Soon, it would be known by the whole city that he had saved them, and all of Aflyr, from the scourge of the Broken Land.

Erik winced as the surgeon pulled a suture closed tightly in his thigh. The man gave him a reassuring smile before pouring hot wine over the wound.

"Your sword not working today?" Braxus asked from the open tent flap.

Erik looked up at the bloodied and bruised mercenary and gave the man a wary smile.

"It has its limits, and so I'm to heal like a common man," Erik offered.

Braxus let out a laugh, "Common men die in the fields without the care of competent surgeons."

"Well said," Erik agreed.

Braxus limped inside and stole a ladle full of hot wine from the surgeon's cook-pot. He took a deep drink, sighed, and then found a place to sit.

"What have you seen from the Ruk encampment?" Erik asked.

"The place is a warren of ankle holes designed to cripple our cavalry, so we were forced to go in on foot which made it all the slower work. We did find the chief's tent we think, and inside there were several large chests filled with loot he must have gained while raiding up the coast," Braxus answered.

"Rings?" Erik asked.

Braxus nodded his head, again taking another ginger sip of the boiled wine. "Four with House Markers in the chests and Lieutenant Gariaus has reported another sixteen in the fields around the city gate."

Erik lifted his head at the mention of Gariaus. The young lieutenant was likable, but he had seen him fall during the battle with the giant Ruk commander and had thought him lost.

"Gariaus is alive?" Erik asked.

Braxus gave a pleased nod. "It looks like he has the blood of a mercenary in him, and the luck as well. He was stitched up by Kin surgeons who found him along the knoll ridge. Once his head cleared up, he jumped back on a horse and returned to his duties."

Erik scratched his chin, "Send word that he is to come here after his duty is complete. I think a promotion to Captain is in order."

Braxus nodded his agreement, and Erik continued, "Eight more rings here on this hill. Do you think that is all of them?"

Braxus shrugged. "Have to ask the Wizard. She's already up in the royal libraries doing whatever it is you asked her to."

Twenty-eight noble signets from the east and ChanderNagor proper. It just might be everything I'd hoped.

"Bloodstar is still going on about the priestess and the Druid, and Igrayn's taken to looking for Tavalori who was lost in that supposed clash of magic," Braxus continued.

"Our scouts haven't seen the priestess then?" Erik asked.

"No. The last person to see her was Bloodstar, and she says the priestess and her mercenary slipped to the East with the young ranger in tow when the chain demon was summoned." Braxus answered.

That is one problem solved, and yet another that may come back to haunt me.

The surgeon finished his work, and began to pack his things, Erik taking a pull on a bottle of wine and motioning to a map on a table nearby.

"The city will be a mess for some time, but some men must be sent back to Mahe. Malcolm is a capable soldier, and I would rather have you here with me as I make my claim."

Braxus grinned and nodded. "As you wish, my Duke."

"That is all I can do," the surgeon interrupted.

Erik looked down at his hip and winced at seeing the stitches.

That will be an ugly scar, but I can't take any magical healing away from men who need it much worse than I. Besides, a scar adds to a man's reputation.

"Well done, Conrad, now please see to my soldiers," Erik said.

The surgeon nodded, finished packing up his things, and then exited the tent without another word.

"The world changes," Erik whispered.

Braxus nodded again and forced his legs back underneath him with a grunt.

"And I have to see that it changes in our favor," the mercenary laughed.

Erik took another long swig as the man limped from the tent.

Let us hope we can pull it off.

"Can I hate you now?" Igrayn asked.

She sat across the fire, her hair down. She was wearing the clothing of a mercenary traveler, not an Arcanian court concubine.

Erik regarded her thoughtfully. When he had finally found time to wander out of his tent to look at what remained of his army, he found her standing like a statue just beyond the horse tethers of the lancers, ghostly beautiful with her breath visible in the moonlight.

"You can." he replied.

She waited, her eyes never leaving his until he sighed and held up his hands. "You know I'm a man of desires, and I had a hand in this, but it was the goddess who tried to play kingmaker today, I just stepped in to fill the role"

"Yet you could have saved the king, and you still held your attack?" she asked.

Erik shook his head, "It has to do with you."

"Me?"

He nodded, "When I found out you were alive, I knew there was still a chance," he continued.

"A chance for what?" she asked, raising her eyebrows.

Erik stared right at her, the air growing moist and hot between them.

"For us to be together," he said.

She shook her head, "I am bound to the King of Aflyr, and no matter whom I choose to sleep with now, it will never change that. No matter how much regicide you deal, you can't change that!"

Erik stared at her, his eyes not leaving hers. As she looked back at him her eyes finally widened even further and she tried to speak but no words came out.

"I knew that moment in the palace, when I saved you from the sorcerer that I wanted you, that I needed you. But it wasn't until Nehru and the promises of Maxus that I understood there might actually be a way to achieve my goal."

"Erik," she whispered, "That isn't possible. You had a hand in murder..."

Her words said one thing, but there was doubt in her tone that echoed like a Delver drum.

"Even as we speak, Telluria is searching the royal libraries against the signets of Aflyrian Nobility that we found on the fields these past few days. If what I think is the case, then so many lines have been lost the only choice the nation can make is to award the crown to the highest ranking, non-royal, blood noble in the country," Erik whispered.

Assuming DeWinter doesn't try to make in-advised claim, and even that can be dealt with.

Igrayn shook her head but he reached out, held her until she stopped moving.

"As Duke of Mahe I hold that title, and with this army I can back my claim against any upstart from here to Nehru," he finished.

For a long moment she stared at him before she croaked his name.

"Erik..." The word was pleading, and her eyes filled with tears.

"I can't take the full burden of this tragedy. Another player was working from the shadows to place their own man on the throne. After I saw their true plot, I simply diverted their plan and made it my own," he said.

Looking down at her he reached up and tipped her chin so that their faces were close.

"Can you forgive me for what I have done?" he asked.

Igrayn's lip quivered, tears falling down her cheeks. Erik could see the conflict inside her. By any definition he had committed dishonorable regicide. He was a Kingslayer. Yet he knew that the king he had allowed to die was a fool whose reign had nearly cost the lives of every man, women and child in Aflyr.

"No," she whispered.

Erik pulled her to him, his arms taking her in, but she pulled away, another scream of 'no' tearing from her throat.

"Is this how it must be then, because you have been as culpable in this result as I," he said.

She shook her head, "No, I was allowed the freedom to do what I chose, but my choices did not knowingly cause the death of anyone."

He nodded, hands coming up to wipe the tears from her eyes but she pulled back again.

"You may have me, Your Grace, but any union with you will be as cold as that of a marriage I would have had to the former king," she choked.

He nodded, and she bowed – without even a hint of irony – before turning and walking into the shifting shadows of soldiers and the lightly falling snow.

A trap of your own making. Yes, you are as grand a fool as anyone ever thought you would become, be you a king or a mercenary...

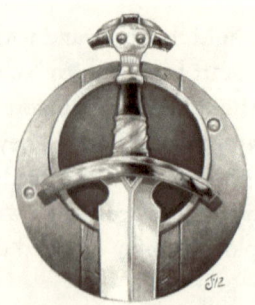

Author Scott Taylor has worked as a writer and editor of both fantasy and science fiction for the past decade. He is currently the Director of Publishing at **Privateer Press** and a blogger for **Black Gate Magazine**. In 2012, he also founded **Art of the Genre**, a **Kickstarter**-based small press that looks to inspire old-school fantasy readers with fast, fun fiction that is illustrated by some of the greatest artists the industry has known over the past thirty years. He currently resides in Ranchos Palos Verdes, California with his wife and son.

Cover artist Jeff Easley is perhaps the greatest fantasy painter of the modern era. He has spent the past thirty years defining fantasy in works like **Dungeons & Dragons**, countless novels, **Magic the Gathering**, and all other manner of fantasy and science fiction art. He currently resides in Lake Geneva, Wisconsin, the birthplace of fantasy role-playing.